WESTWARD THE WAGONS

They were on their way to California—men, women and children with all their worldly goods, crossing the western plains by covered wagon.

Bill Raines, young leader of the wagon train, knew they were carrying $86,000 in cash. McBride's gang knew it too, and they'd stop at nothing to get it. Only Raines could save the wagon train from the vicious outlaws' greed!

WESTWARD THE WAGONS

Burt and Budd Arthur

WESTERNS

First published 1957
by Tower Publications Inc.

This hardback edition 1992
by Chivers Press
by arrangement with
Donald MacCampbell, Inc.

ISBN 0 7451 4516 7

British Library Cataloguing in Publication Data available

Printed and bound in Great Britain by
Redwood Press Limited, Melksham, Wiltshire

CHAPTER I

IT WAS the middle of the afternoon of a long, wearying day in July. It had been a thoroughly hot day too, beginning with a sticky, sweaty dawn that eventually became a muggy morning and noon. And now, hours later, the air was stiflingly oppressive. heavy with heat that seemed to rise up out of the earth and the grass and form a vapoury haze that stretched steadily upwards like a gauzy curtain until it was lost from sight. Northwards, beyond the haze, were the Big Horn Mountains; southwards and only faintly visible was the etched outline of a chain of stubby, rugged hills that someone had curiously and inexplicably named the Front Range. Wyoming summers and winters were known to be extreme and toll exacting. Hence it was not to be expected that heat-seared or half-frozen travellers, cursing the elements for conspiring against them as they wended their way across country, should give any thought to the Front Range or why it bore such an old name. They accepted it without comment and manifested no interest in it. Between the Big Horn and the Front was a gap, a ten-mile-wide expanse of green-and-brown tinged, hump-backed open country, the only negotiable east-west passage for wagon trains.

Dust clouds arose and billowed upwards into the placid blue sky, opened gently and drifted away and soon dissolved into nothingness. The source and cause of the dust was a wagon train. Actually it was a double line of wagons, cumbersome, top-heavy, canvas-topped prairie schooners, with each line at least a quarter of a mile long, and both lines lumbering along with less than a dozen feet of searing sunlight between them. The train was heading for a grassy slope, the far side of which led downwards on to a flat tableland that was the north-easterly corner of Utah. The train's route skirted the great desert, then swung southwards along the mythical Utah-Nevada State line, then out westward again, directly across Nevada, first to Virginia City, then a bit southwardly to Carson City, and on into California. There the train would break up, with the gold seekers striking northwards through the Yosemite Valley to Sacramento and points farther north, and the settlers, the farmers from Ohio and Illinois, turning their wagons towards the fertile and flowered valleys to the south.

Dust swirled and spiralled skywards from the huge wagon wheels and the horses' hooves as the train forged

over the plain to the foot of the slope. The lead wagon
mounted the incline. The panting, heaving, sweated horses
pulling the wagon dug their hooves into the sides of the
slope and the lurching wagon began to crunch upwards.
A whip snaked out over the struggling horses' heads and
cracked with the echoing report of a pistol shot; the
schooner swayed a little drunkenly when one of its front
wheels collided with a half-buried rock, finally ground
over it and came thudding down again with a jarring
effect on the wagon. Axles, shaft and harness creaked
dismally, and the horses wheezed nasally as they plodded
upwards. A couple of horsemen rode up, swung themselves down from their mounts, ran to the wagon and put
their shoulders to it. The wheels turned and the wagon
tongue jutted out ahead of the horses and dragged them
along. The wagon reached the halfway mark, then the
three-quarters point, and finally, with the horses' tongues
hanging out of their lathered mouths, it topped the crest,
rolled down the far side of the slope and braked raspingly
to a stop. The horses, their legs wide-spread, their heads
bowed and their matted sides heaving, took advantage of
the respite to blow themselves.

A second wagon had already started up the slope. A
lean, unusually youthful looking rider astride a nimble-
footed horse jogged up the grassy incline, passed the
climbing wagon, reached the top of the slope and rode
down the far side. He glanced at the man and the bon-
neted woman who occupied the driver's seat of the halted
wagon, and loped past them. They followed him with
their eyes, saw him stop short of the bottom of the downgrade, hand-shade his eyes and scan the countryside.

John Anderson, shifting the reins in his big hands, answered his wife's unasked question.

"He's just taking a look around to see that everything's all right before he gives us the signal to go on," he said.

"Oh," Mary Anderson said simply.

Her husband held his gaze on the horseman below them squinted a little because of the sun.

"Will Cather seems to think that young feller knows a heap about this part of the country," he went on shortly. "I sure hope so. Nobody else knows where we are. Every morning I have to ask Will if we're still in Wyoming and if he thinks we'll ever get to California. He turns to that young feller and waits for him to answer me."

"Think I heard someone say his name is Raines."

"Yes. Bill Raines."

The second wagon came lumbering up to the top of the slope, rolled over it and started down the far side. The Andersons watched it go past and pull up just beyond them. A third and fourth wagon climbed the slope, then a fifth. Then they came rolling up, one hard behind the other until there were eleven of then strung out on the downgrade. Raines wheeled around, rode up the slope and halted near the Anderson wagon. A big man mounted on a sweating horse pulled up alongside of Raines and eased himself in the saddle.

"How's it look, Bill?" the Andersons heard him ask.

"All right, Will," Raines replied. "How much further you planning to go on for today?"

Cather glanced skywards.

"I think this will be it for today," he said. "We'll make camp down below and stay put till the storm blows over."

"Storm?" Raines repeated.

He looked at Cather obliquely, and when he lifted his gaze skywards, Cather grinned.

"You won't find any sign of it up there," he said. "Broke my leg a couple of years ago when my horse fell and threw me and rolled over on me." Raines looked at him again. Cather tapped his right thigh with a thick finger. "This one. Ever since I've been able to tell what kind of weather we're going to have by the way my leg feels. And it's aching right now."

He wheeled away from Raines, twisted around in the saddle and yelled, "All right, folks! Let's go!"

The wagon horses stirred themselves reluctantly. Wagons creaked as their wheels began to turn and crunch. One by one the top-heavy schooners got under way again and followed Cather down the slope to the flatland below it. Raines looked skywards again. A black cloud was beginning to form overhead. He shook his head and muttered, "The son-uva-gun." He rode down the slope and halted at Cather's side.

"See it?" the latter asked.

"Y'mean that black cloud?"

"Uh-huh. Hope we get all the wagons down here before the storm hits."

Wagon after wagon topped the incline and made its way down the side to join those being guided into camp position by Cather. Raines rode up the slope and pulling up at the top watched the climbing wagons negotiate the upgrade. The last six wagons in the train were making their way up when the rain burst upon them. There was a distant rumbling in the darkening sky, a sudden frightening clap of thunder and the downpour, a pelting, punishing, swirling rain that turned the grassy incline into a quagmire. A wagon halfway up the slope stopped and suddenly began to roll downhill. when one of its horses lost its footing and fell. There was a scream of terror from a woman when the mate to the hapless horse panicked and found itself being dragged down the slope by the heavy wagon. There were shouts and cries and yells, all of them adding to the confusion and excitement. Then there was a loud agonising splintering sound indicating that the shaft had snapped off. Despite the weight of its horses, the hurtling wagon seemed to gather momentum as it careened down the slope. The wagons behind it struggled frantically to pull out of its path. A couple of them succeeded. But others found the slippery footing too much for them. Terrified horses scrambled this way and that, and the plunging wagon, swinging around, crashed into two other wagons. The three swayed together for a moment like a trio of great bulls or buffaloes with their horns locked together. Then two wagons toppled over to the accompaniment of screams. while the third wagon promptly collided with a fourth and sent it reeling into a fifth. The last wagon. turning aside desperately, was side-swiped and crashed over on its side. A huge wheel came rolling down the slope and hurtled into a team of panicked horses. There was a frenzied cry. the pained screech of an injured animal. and the wagon behind tottered unsteadily. The canvas top collapsed on the heads of the people inside.

Bill Raines caught a fleeting glimpse of a girl's face somewhere in the crush of wagons. Her cheeks were

blood-drained and ashen white, her eyes wide and re-
flecting terror. He flung himself off his horse and went
plunging down the slope, skidded past a lurching wagon
that threatened to overturn, barely managed to swerve
away from the threshing legs of a downed, pain-wracked
horse, reached the girl's wagon and leaped recklessly for
the seat. He made it somehow, miraculously, struck and
caromed off the girl, ripped the reins out of her hands
and with one backward sweep of his arm brushed her
back off the seat. She disappeared behind him inside
the wagon. By this time, though other men had taken a
hand in the melee; rough, strong hands brought terror-
stricken horses to a stop. There was some trampling
and bumping, but the situation was soon brought under
control.

Raines swung around on the seat and peered into the
shadowy depths of the wagon. There were pieces of fur-
niture, a couple of up-ended barrels and a handful of
boxes at the rear. Whoever had stowed them away had
wedged them in so tightly that they had withstood the
jouncing on the slope. But the smaller and lighter things,
pots and pans and bits of clothing, were strewn about on
the wagon. By this time, though, other men had taken a
half-opened blanket roll among the other things. But
there was no sign of the girl.

"Hey," he said. "You can come out now."

There was no response. He frowned, dropped down
into the wagon and almost stepped on a huddled, hunched-
over figure that lay on the floor directly below the driver's
seat. Quickly he knelt down. It was the white-faced girl.
He eased her over on her back, crooked his arm under

11

her head and raised it a bit. Something swung and thumped against his shoulder and he turned his head to see what it was. It was a canteen, and he could hear water sloshing around in it as it swung back and forth from a nail in the nearest canvas stave. He ripped it off the nail and managed to uncork it with his free hand. He forced some water into the girl's mouth, prying her lips apart with his thumb. Some of the water trickled down her chin and dropped on the tight bodice of her dress. Her eyelids fluttered. Her eyes opened and fixed themselves on his face. He smiled at her and some colour surged back into her cheeks.

"All right now?" he asked.

Her eyes shifted a bit, for only a moment though, from his sun-bronzed face to his white, even teeth; then they came up again to his face.

"I . . . I think so," she replied somewhat hesitantly. She moved her head a little and the motion made her wince. "My head hurts. I must have bumped it."

"Yeah, guess you did," he said wryly. "I must have pushed you harder than I realised. Y'see, I was afraid you'd get thrown off the seat in all that milling around, and when I jumped up on the seat I had to do things in a hurry. I'm sorry I was so rough."

"The chances are I'd have got lots worse than a mere bump if you hadn't acted so quickly," she said with a wan smile. "It took a lot of nerve to do what you did."

He reached for the blanket roll, brought it closer and flipped it open, lifted her off the floor and on to the blanket.

"You stay put there for now," he instructed her. "When

we get straightened out, we'll have a look at your head."

She had already taken notice that his shirt and neckerchief were drenched; his hat was wet, too, but he had pushed it back on his head to prevent the water from dripping on her. He held up the canteen.

"Want some more?" he asked.

"No, thank you."

He corked the canteen and slung it up on the nail and got up on his feet. When he straightened up he bumped his head on the top curve of the stave. He frowned again and climbed up on the seat. She heard the hand brake screech as he released it. There was a creaking, dismal squealing sound as the wagon moved. As it resumed its uphill climb, it jounced and swayed and she winced and closed her eyes tightly. That was all she remembered until she was startled into awakening by the feeling that the rain was beating down upon her. She tried to twist away from it, but something held her fast. She opened her eyes to see what it was. She was lying on her side facing the wall of the wagon and her face was barely an inch from the wall. But she was wet. There wasn't any doubt of it. That is, her face and her wrists were wet. She slumped down on her back. Then she saw him again. He was kneeling beside her, and in his hand was a water-soaked piece of white cloth with which he had been bathing her face and wrists.

"Oh," she said.

"Guess you passed out when we were making it up the hill," he explained. "Feel stronger now?"

"Oh, yes," she assured him.

"If you think you'll be all right by yourself for a few

minutes, I'll go see if I can rustle up some hot coffee. That ought to fix you up."

A strand of damp hair dropped limply on her cheek and he tucked it back in place very gravely with a big finger.

"May I sit up now, please?"

He considered for a moment, then he shook his head.

"No, I don't think you ought to," he said. "Be better if you stay put like you are till I get back. Oughtn't to take me more than a couple of minutes."

He tossed the wet cloth up on the seat. Then he got up on his feet, straightened up forgetfully and promptly bumped his head on the stave. He frowned, bent his head and took off his hat and touched his head gingerly.

"We'll have to do something about that," he said. "Before I get my brains knocked out." A faint smile of amusement toyed briefly at the corners of her mouth. He put on his hat. "Be right back."

It was five minutes later when he returned.

"Coffee isn't ready yet," he told her as he climbed over the seat and down into the wagon. He produced a flask of whisky, uncorked it and held it out to her. "Take a swallow of that."

"No, thank you."

"Go on," he urged. "A little swallow of it can't hurt you."

"I know. But I'd rather not."

He didn't press the matter. He corked the flask and returned it to his hip pocket.

"Has the rain stopped?" she asked. "I don't hear it beating down on the canvas."

"Stopped a couple of minutes ago," he answered. "But

It did enough damage while it lasted. Cost us nine horses and four wagons and scared the daylights out've half a dozen women and some of them just about set to have babies. And then as if that wasn't enough, Will Cather got himself banged up."

She looked concerned.

"Seriously?"

"No," he said. "His horse got tangled up with a couple of others and Will got himself spilled. But he'll be up and around again by morning, and outside of feeling a little stiff and sore, he'll probably be as chipper as ever. Right now he's laying down in the Anderson wagon with Missus Anderson ridin' hard on him and refusing to let him budge out've there till morning."

She nodded understandingly and looked relieved.

"We're staying put here for tonight," he continued. "Meanwhile I'll have to take care of things for Will. Not that there's anything special I have to do. Just see that everything's under control. Think you'll be all right for a while?"

"Of course."

"I had a look at that lump you got on your head," he said. "It's a beaut, all right But I don't think there's anything we can do about it. Chances are the swelling will be down by morning anyway." He turned slowly, carefully too, eyeing the stave on which he had twice bumped his head. "When I get back we'll eat."

After he had gone, she struggled up into a sitting position But her head ached so, she was quite content to sink down again on the blanket. After a while her eyes closed. She did not intend to sleep; however, unwillingly or otherwise, she dozed off only to wake with a start when she heard something fall close by. Raines looked down at her and grinned.

"Had to drop that danged plate and spoil things," she heard him say ruefully. "Good thing the bacon was on the other plate."

She sat up at once.

"Um," she said. "Bacon. And it smells heavenly."

"Hope it tastes as good," he said. He sank down beside her in a cross-legged squat and placed a well-filled tin plate of crisp bacon on the floor between them. "We don't need that other plate, the one I dropped and kicked around, do we?"

"I don't," she answered.

"I know I don't," he said. "Oh, want your coffee now or afterwards?"

"I think I'd like it now, please," she said and added: "If it isn't too much trouble."

He twisted around She hadn't noticed the pot standing on the floor almost directly beneath the lip of the seat, or the two tin cups flanking it. He filled both cups and handed her one. She smiled her thanks.

"It smells awfully good," she said. She sipped her coffee, raised her eyes to him and announced quite simply: "It is good."

He nodded and said, "Dig into the bacon."

He held his gaze on her while she ate a small, curled-up piece, and finally asked: "All right?"

"Oh, yes! In fact, it's just about the best I've ever eaten."

Apparently satisfied, he selected a piece of bacon for himself, lifted it to his mouth with his fingers, munched it slowly and washed it down with some coffee. He shoved his hat back on his head, finally took it off and slung it aside. She was studying him over the rim of her cup. He was big and his arm and shoulder muscles rippled whenever he moved. He was rather nice looking she had already decided; now that she could study him more closely she felt she had done him an injustice. He was very good looking. She smiled suddenly and he eyed her quizzically.

"I was just thinking," she said. "We're sitting here so unconventionally, yet we don't even know each other. What's your name?"

"Raines. Bill Raines."

"Where do you come from?"

"California."

"What do you do?"

"Haven't been doing anything much these last two years," he told her. "Before that I worked on a ranch. My father's."

She made no comment, waited instead for him to go on.

"Mom got sick and died," he continued, "and Pop's heart got tired and quit on him. With both of them gone, I kinda lost interest in things, closed up the place, and we-ll, now I'm home wherever I find a place to bed down."

"That isn't a very satisfactory way to live, is it?"

"It's anything but," he answered quite frankly.

"Don't you ever get the urge to stop wandering and go home where you belong, where your roots are?"

"That's why I took this job with Cather And once we hit California, that will be it for me. It will be home, sweet home for me, and I'll stay put there. I think I've got the foot-loose feeling out've my system for good."

17

They sat in silence, thoughtful, eyes-averted silence for a long moment. Then he looked up again.

"How come you're making this trip yourself?" he asked.

"There wasn't anyone else to make it with," she replied.

"You mean . . . "

"I haven't a family either."

"That's tough. A heap tougher on a girl than on a man. What are you planning to do when we get to California?"

"Work."

"Where?"

"Wherever I can get a job."

"What do you do?"

"The usual thing. I'm a schoolteacher. But I've other kinds of experience, too. I've clerked in a store and I've worked in a bank, and my last job was keeping books for an express company. Oh, yes . . . I had a new career offered me just before I left home."

"That so?"

"Yes. Some man who was trying to interest some girls in going to California to marry miners offered to take me along too."

"Uh-huh. But you turned him down."

She nodded and indulged herself in a tiny, almost wistful smile.

"I think I'd like to do my own choosing of a husband," she said. "Not have someone else do it for me. I can't imagine getting to California with a number pinned on me and having some man, a total stranger and one whom I'd probably dislike on sight, rush up to me, grab me and holler: 'Are you number such-and-such? Good. That's my

number on the list, so that makes you the bride I'm supposed to get.' O-h, no . . . that isn't for me."

There was a sudden clatter of hooves and a horseman
jerked to a stop beside the wagon, stood up and peered
in.

"Hey, Raines!" he called. "You in there?"

Raines put down his cup, got to his feet and leaned
over the driver's seat.

"Yeah?" he asked.

"We're getting company," the man said. "Six men are
riding this way. Somebody said you're in charge while
Cather's laid up, so I figured you'd want to know."

Raines swung himself over the seat and climbed down
to the ground.

CHAPTER II

DESPITE the cushioning effect of the soggy ground, there was a carrying drum of approaching hooves as the oncoming band of six strung-out horsemen neared the halted train. When Raines stepped away from the girl's wagon, the mounted man who had summoned him moved with him and now stood at his side. The man in the lead of the band held up his hand as he slowed his own horse and the men behind him drew rein too. They pulled up a dozen feet from the train and formed a somewhat uneven half-circle and slacked in their saddles while their leader, a burly, stubble-faced individual walked his horse up to Raines. The latter, standing slightly spread-legged, with his thumbs hooked in his belt, lifted his eyes to the burly man.

"Howdy."

"Howdy," Raines responded.

A bold, insolent, almost challenging gaze held for a moment on Raines in unconcealed appraisal, then it shifted to the horseman at Raines' side, then back again to Raines.

"Where'll I find the head man?"

"He isn't around," Raines answered. "Something I can do for you?"

"N-o, I don't think so. We know this country and we kinda think your boss might be interested in hiring us to guide you folks."

"I'm doing that," Raines said quietly.

The burly man smiled. When his thick lips eased back, his teeth showed, short, stubby and yellowish, and black at the gum line.

"I mean to California, sonny Think we'll make our-selves comfortable and wait around till your boss shows up and put it up to him. Where's the chow wagon?"

"There isn't any."

The man frowned. He twisted around in the saddle.

"Get down, boys," he called. "We're staying."

He swung himself off his horse, hitched up his belt and shifted his holster a little. He stopped abruptly and looked up again when there was movement behind Raines. The girl appeared, poked her head out above the wide seat. The stubble-faced man stared a little, then a smile parted his lips, and his eyes shone.

"Well, what d'you know?" He half-turned and called: "Hey, Pete! Looks like my luck's still good. Take a look at what's waiting for Poppa up in that wagon!"

His companions had dismounted as he had instructed them. One of the five, apparently the one named Pete, a wiry, leather-faced man who wore a low-slung Colt in a cutaway holster riding on his right thigh, laughed and sauntered forward. The burly man laughed too, hitched up his belt again, moved past Raines to the wagon and put his foot on the hub of the front wheel and reached for the seat to pull himself up. Raines caught him by the arm, stopping him, and pulling him down.

"Stay out've there," he said curtly.

The man levelled a long look at him, and with a sudden sweep of his right arm pushed off Raines' hand. Then, pivoting with surprising agility for one of his bulk, he swung mightily at Raines. But Raines' movement was even swifter, so lightning-like, it was almost incredible. There was a sharp, echoing crack, the sickening impact of a sledge-hammer fist colliding with bone, and the man fell against the wheel. He slid down to his knees and clung to the wooden spokes with both hands. Slowly he dragged himself up again as Raines, watching him alertly, backed off a couple of steps. The mounted man who had been sitting quietly at Raines' side, backed his horse away too. The burly man was up now, his thick shoulders hunched, his head thrust forward and his fists balled up. With a sudden bellow he hurled himself at Raines. The girl, peering out with wide eyes, saw Raines meet him head-on. There was an exchange of punches, a thud each time one landed, and she turned her head.

"Get up," she heard a voice say curtly, a voice that she recognised at once as Raines', and she looked down again quickly.

The big man lay sprawled out on his face in the trampled grass and churned-up dirt with his bent arms and half-clenched fists encircling his bare head. His hat, a battered, dust-coated thing, lay near him. Pete had halted a couple of feet away and stood looking down at him with his hands on his hips and a curious half-smile on his thin face. Obviously, though, the scornful twist to his lips was not intended for Raines, for he did not look at him. It was plain his contempt was meant for the man whom Raines had beaten down. Raines glanced at Pete, then he shot a quick look at the four men who were idling at the heads of their horses. They gave no sign that they intended to take a hand in the little drama that was being enacted before their eyes. Satisfied then that they would not interfere, Raines held his full gaze on the man who lay at his feet. The man stirred and forced himself up to his hands and knees.

There was a sudden rush of booted feet and a dozen rifle-armed train men with Cather at the head of them, clutching a half-raised black Colt in his hand, came pounding up. Cather skidded to a stop and his men crowded around behind him. He looked questioningly at Raines' victim, then at Raines.

"What in blazes is going on here?" he demanded. But before Raines could answer, Cather, levelling a hard look at Pete, asked grumpily: "Who are you?"

Pete smiled thinly.

"Who, me?"

"Yeah, you!" Cather fairly spat at him.

Raines, hitching up his levis and tucking in his shirt-tail at almost the same time, moved away from the man on the ground.

"His name is Lopat," he said with a nod in Pete's direction. "He's a hired gun, with such a reputation for killing for pay, there isn't a lawman from Texas to the Dakotas who wouldn't give his eye-teeth to get a rope around Mister Lopat's neck."

Lopat laughed lightly, and Cather, jerking his head

23

around, stared at him.

"And that maverick," Raines went on, indicating with another nod the burly man who had got to his feet and who was now standing on wide-spread, unsteady legs. There was an angry red scrape on his jaw, a blood smear on his lips and blood bubbles in his nostrils. "His name is McBride. The law's looking for him too. He specialises in robbing small wagon trains. Understand the law in Oklahoma nearly had him hanged once. But something happened and he got away. But the next time they catch up with him they'll fix him good. They'll really stretch his neck for him."

Cather raised his gun.

"All right, you buzzards," he said curtly, and his Colt moved in an arc that took in both Lopat and McBride. "Get up on your horses and get going. We don't like your kind around our wagons."

Lopat turned slowly and walked back to his horse and climbed up astride the animal. McBride wiped his mouth with the back of his grimy hands, and in turn wiped his hand on his pants' leg. He glared at Raines.

"Go on, you," Cather ordered, holding his gun on McBride. "Get out've here and don't come back. If you do, we'll give you something you won't forget in a hurry. Go on now. Move."

He took a step towards McBride. The battered man turned and lumbered over to his horse, hauled himself up into the saddle with an effort and wheeled away. He jogged past his waiting companions who had already mounted and they rode after him. Only Lopat lingered behind. Sitting his horse a little off to a side, he looked at Raines and when he caught the tall youth's eye, he smiled his crooked little smile and said:

"I'll be seeing you, Mister."

Will Cather bristled.

"If we see you first, you murderin' polecat," he yelled, "we'll do the job for the law and for free!"

Lopat laughed again, swung his horse around and loped away.

Cather, angry looking and red-faced, followed Lopat with his eyes. When the gunman had ridden out of sight, Cather lowered his Colt, shoved it down inside the waistband of his pants.

"All right, men," he said, turning to the train men who had held their rifles on Lopat and the others in McBride's gang. "It's all over. Go back to your wagons and to your womenfolk. They're probably stewin' and frettin' because I made them take cover instead of letting them stick their noses in here to see what was up. So g'wan back to them and relieve their minds."

When he gestured, the men backed off, turned and trudged away. After they had gone, Cather levelled a long look at Raines.

"Well?" he demanded.

"Well, what?"

"Think you can keep the peace for a spell if I go back and lay down again?"

"I'll try," Raines answered gravely. "But I can't give you a guarantee."

"What'd you hit that McBride with?"

Raines held up his right fist. The knuckles were red, the skin over them scraped and torn.

"H'm," Cather said. "You did a pretty good job on him with that. But next time use a club. You'll do an even better job."

"I'll try to remember that."

"Bill, you think they'll come back?"

"No. We've got too many guns for them. Of course, if they can tie up with another bunch like themselves, and there are supposed to be a lot of gangs like McBride's roaming the range, that will be another story. Then you can bet on it they'll come calling again."

"Then we can't take any chances. We'd better be ready for them just in case."

"That's right, Will."

"Outriders in the daytime and we'd better double the guards at night."

"If they come again, it won't be in the daytime. We'll be shooting from behind cover and that will be too much of an advantage. So they'll come at night and hope to take us by surprise."

"Can I leave it to you for tonight to see that they don't jump us when we aren't prepared for them?"

"Sure, Will."

Shoving his gun down a little deeper inside his waistband, Cather trudged away.

Raines climbed into the wagon. The girl was sitting quietly on the blanket. He sat down facing her, cross-legged as before. He reached for the coffee pot, hefted it, and when he heard coffee swish around in the pot, he nodded, suddenly turned his head, looked at the girl and asked. "What'd you say your name was?"

She smiled a little wanly. "I didn't."

"Hey, that's right. We were coming to it when we were interrupted " He looked hard at her. "What's the matter?"

"Nothing."

26

"Come on now. The way you were looking at me, I couldn't tell whether I'd done something I shouldn't have, or the other way round."

She shook her head.

"No," she said. "It wasn't anything you did or didn't do. I was just wondering. That's all."

"Oh," he said. "Wondering about what?"

"Those men," she said simply.

"You mean if they'll come back?"

"Yes."

"I don't think so. But if they do, we'll take care of them. We've got men and we've got guns. So you don't have to worry. That's the advantage of being with a big train There are always plenty of men and guns and even McBride wouldn't want to bite off a bigger piece than he can chew. It might choke him. So I don't think you have to worry your pretty head about him. Now d'you think you might break down and tell me what your name is? Or d'you want me to just call you 'You' or 'Hey, you'?"

"I don't think I'd care for either of those. My name's Margaret. Margaret Taylor. But everyone who knows me calls me Peggy."

"Peggy, huh?"

He poured a cupful of coffee for himself, sipped some of it and said: "It isn't hot. But it's still warm enough."

"Don't you like Peggy?"

"Oh, sure," he answered He put down his cup, looked at her for a long moment, finally grinned and said: "If you ever give me a hard time, y'know what I'm going to call you?"

"What?" she insisted upon knowing.

27

"Maggie, that's what! Come on, let me have your cup."

* * *

The transition from dusk to evening to night was amazingly swift on the open range. There was a barely discernible interval between them. It was surprising, too, how suddenly the day's intense heat, admittedly lessened somewhat by the storm, dissolved in the gathering darkness. Then, almost before anyone fully realised it, there was a distinct chill in the air. A stiffening breeze came sweeping down from the Big Horn, obscured by the darkness. Loose canvas wagon flaps slapped against the wooden sides. Limp bits of twigs, grass and flower petals and sun-scorched leaves and then dust swirled around in the wake of the breeze; when it died down or swerved away southwardly, they dropped soundlessly to the ground. The pale blue of the sky deepened into a rich velvety hue, and the sky itself was brilliantly alight as bright, eager stars appeared and twinkled against the blue background. Then the moon made its appearance and in its fullest glory and the night was complete.

With the advent of night, a deep restful silence blanketed the wagon train. Since strict orders forbidding the showing of lights had been issued, the train was draped in darkness. The horses, having been fed and watered, had been unhitched, backed inside the outer wall of wagons and tied up to the wheels of their respective wagons. They were too tired to mill about as they usually did; instead they huddled together in bowed silence. Their equally tired owners had turned in, and now, save for the men on guard, everyone was asleep. Peggy Taylor was among them.

"Bill," she had asked as Raines prepared to leave her

wagon after they had had their supper, "You meant that, didn't you, about the chances of those men coming back again?"

"Y'mean McBride and his outfit? 'Course I meant it."

"And you weren't just saying that so I wouldn't worry?"

"I said I don't think they'll come back and that's exactly what I meant."

She stood at the seat and watched him climb up and over it, balancing tin dishes and cups in one hand and the empty coffee pot in the other.

"Thanks for everything," she had said with a grateful smile.

He had grinned back at her.

"Sure. See you tomorrow," he had responded over his shoulder. And then, when he had safely managed to reach the ground without mishap, he had turned and looked up at her again. It was too dark for him to see her face. But he knew she was still there. "When I get done with things and I get a chance to curl up in my blanket, I'll be right here under your wagon. So you won't be alone."

"Good night, Bill," the faceless shadowy figure that was Peggy Taylor answered.

"Night, Peggy."

He heard the canvas drop-curtain slither down behind the seat and shut out the night and he strode away.

CHAPTER III

THE KURT HEYDRICH family occupied two wagons in the middle of the train. Kurt, a big, heavily-muscled man who was slow of speech and deliberate of movement, drove the first Heydrich wagon. His wife, Anna, who was blonde and buxom and who wore her braided hair wound around her head, drove the second wagon. The Heydrich's were farmers, originally from German Saxony, and more recently from Illinois. Kurt was the stolid, phlegmatic type, expressionless and totally un-imaginative; Anna was just the opposite. She laughed and sang a great deal, but despite her gaiety she was smart and shrewd and decidedly far-seeing The Heydrichs' daughter, Katrina, was blonde like her mother, but unlike Anna she was supple and graceful. Katrina rode in the second wagon with Anna.

It was early the next morning and Katrina was dressing behind the drop-curtain. She lifted a corner of it and peeked out once. It was bright and sunny outside and the air smelled good and clean. She noticed, too, that for a change there was no morning haze. She let the curtain fall back in place and went on buttoning up her dress.

Anna, who was an early riser, had just finished backing the horses into the traces and was about to hitch them up when she heard the soft thump of approaching hooves. She peered out and saw Bill Raines coming slowly down the line of awakening wagons. As he came abreast of her Anna looked up and smiled; he acknowledged gravely by touching the brim of his hat. As he jogged past, Anna followed him with appraising eyes. She did not turn when she heard the heavy step of someone coming towards her. She knew it was Kurt. It was only when he came up beside her that she turned to him.

"Kurt," she said, "I think our Katrina should know that young man."

He looked at her blankly.

"Which young man?"

"You did not see him ride by?"

"No."

Anna looked annoyed. Her strong hands reached out and curled around Kurt's arms and she turned him around and pointed down the line.

"That young man," she said. "The one on the horse."

"Oh," Kurt said. "His name is Raines."

"If that is his name, so?"

"Nothing," Kurt said. "But why should Katrina know him?"

"Because he is the kind of young man Katrina should marry," Anna said simply.

Kurt looked at her oddly.

"You can tell that just by looking at him?"

"A woman can tell a lot by looking at a man."

31

Kurt shrugged his shoulder.

"I want you should stop him when he rides back," Anna went on.

"And then?"

"Never mind about 'and then.' I will talk to him."

"But what will you talk to him about?"

"I will think of something."

It did not make sense to Kurt and the expression on his face showed it.

"If you wish it, Anna, all right. I will do it. But I do not like this kind of business. Besides, maybe he is already married. What then?"

Anna shook her head.

"He is not married," she stated with finality.

"You can tell that, too, just by looking at him?"

"No. I asked Will Cather and he told me."

"Oh," Kurt said. "What do you think Katrina would say about this business?"

"What could she say?"

"I am asking you that," Kurt said. "You know, Anna, sometimes you are a very strange woman. Sometimes I do not understand you."

"If you were a mother and you had a daughter who was already nineteen years old, you would understand everything."

"But since I am only the father . . . "

"Only the father?" Anna echoed. "A father is very important."

"I am very glad," Kurt said dryly.

"Only a father is just a man, so what can a daughter expect of him? Oh, I know. You have been a good father to Katrina. She has never wanted for anything. But

32

that is not enough for a girl. She looks to her mother for the important things, the things a man does not understand."

"What is more important than a good home, good food to eat, good clothes to wear?"

"You see, Kurt, you do not understand."

"So?"

"So nothing."

"Tell me," Kurt began again. "What is to be about Karl Linden? I always thought that same day Katrina and he would . . . "

"Karl is in Illinois," Anna said. "And this is Wyoming, and soon we will be in California."

"So?"

"Katrina will probably never see him again. And maybe that is a good thing."

Kurt looked surprised.

"But I thought you liked Karl."

"Karl is a very nice young man, but he is not for our daughter. If we were still in Germany, maybe I would say 'yes'. In America, 'no'. Karl does not like it here. He does not like Americans or American ways. We do. So does Katrina."

"So?"

"So the young man Katrina marries must be an American; and that young man, that Raines, he is American. That is why I want Katrina should meet him."

Kurt made no comment.

"Quick," Anna said suddenly. "He is coming."

She turned away from her husband to the idling horses and started to hitch them to the shafts. Kurt stepped out as Raines jogged up.

33

"Good morning," Kurt said politely.

"Morning," Bill responded.

Kurt shot a quick glance over his shoulder at Anna; in that moment Raines had ridden past. Anna wheeled like a flash.

"Mister Raines," she called.

Bill jerked his mount to a stop, twisted around and looked back. Anna smiled at him. He looked at her for a moment; then he wheeled his horse and rode back.

"Did you call me, ma'am?" he asked.

Kurt looked quickly at Anna, wondering what she was going to say.

"Yes," she said, still smiling. Her calmness amazed Kurt. "When you rode by just now, I almost thought you were my brother." Kurt swallowed hard. "He is so much like you, tall and young and handsome—just like you."

Raines grinned boyishly.

"Aw, now."

"My brother's name is Fritz," Anna added. "In America it would be Fred, no?"

"Yeah, I guess it would."

There was a dimple in Anna's round cheek; the dimple always appeared when she smiled deeply. There was a coyness in the way she cocked her head to one side and looked up at him.

"Perhaps you will have breakfast with us?" she asked.

"That's mighty nice of you, Missus . . . "

"Heydrich," Anna said gently.

Kurt's eyes shifted from one to the other.

"Missus Heydrich," Bill said. "But the fact is, ma'am, I've got a heap of things to do before I can even think of

34

breakfast. But it was swell of you to ask me, and I sure appreciate it."

He wheeled his horse. The canvas drop-curtain was suddenly whipped back and a girl appeared in front of it. Raines' horse stopped in its tracks. Anna, watching him, saw the tall youth's eyes widen; satisfied, Anna turned and looked up at her daughter. Katrina had never shown to better advantage. The bright morning sun made her blonde hair look golden, and her eyes had never been more blue. Her full, rounded cheeks were flushed, and when her eyes fell with maidenly modesty before Raines', Anna smiled approvingly.

"This is my daughter, Katrina," Anna said. "Katrina, this is Mr. Raines."

"Just make it Bill, ma'am," Raines said.

Quite properly, there was no actual reply from Katrina; nothing but a shy glance at him, a quick, fleeting smile, then another maidenly blush. Anna was quite pleased with her daughter.

"Katrina," Anna began.

"Mama, please," a voice that was like Anna's but twenty years younger said. "Katey, Mama. Remember?"

Anna laughed lightly.

"Ach, I am ashamed that I always forget. Katey, maybe if you would ask Mr. Raines he would stay and have breakfast with us. Yes?"

"Mama, Mr. Raines . . . "

"Bill," Raines said.

The girl raised her head and smiled.

"Bill," she said, looking at him; then she looked at Anna. "Bill has told you already that he can't stay. We must not press him and embarrass him, you know."

"Thanks," Bill said. "But look—does that invite hold good for some other time, too?"

"Of course."

"Fine. I'll remember it."

Bill touched his hat gravely, nudged his horse with his knees and rode away. Anna and Katey followed him with their eyes; when he swung in between a couple of wagons far up the line, Anna turned to her daughter and smiled.

"He is nice—no?"

"Very nice, Mama."

"So he is nice," Kurt said. "Good. Now maybe we could have some breakfast? Yes?"

* * *

The train did not move that day.

At nine o'clock that morning the first of the new babies was born. The second one appeared approximately an hour later, and the third kicked its way into the world at noon. There was a great deal of grim-faced scurrying about by the other women in the train who knew exactly what to do. Meanwhile, their husbands lounged around, patiently and understandingly at first; when the time began to drag, they began to get restless and impatient. When the word was passed around that one of the new mothers, a Mrs. Archer, was very ill, and that it might be necessary for the train to lay-over for a couple of days, some of the more impatient men looked annoyed. The farmers in the party seemed to be more patient than the others; they appeared to understand the need for rest and quiet for the new mothers. They accepted the situation with a shrug which meant that they hoped the lay-over would not be too long. Loud-voiced protests were raised by a group of gold hunters, who, as soon as they learned of what they considered an unscheduled halt and therefore an unnecessary one, staged an impromptu meeting that resulted in the formation of a three-man committee that was instructed to see Cather at once and demand that the train go on without further delay. Headed by a lean, sour-faced man named Hammond, the trio went striding up the line to the Andersons' wagon and clamoured for Cather to come out. After a few minutes' wait, Cather appeared. The other people in the train pushed forward in order to hear the discussion. Cather listened to Hammond for about a minute, then stopped him abruptly.

"You've said just about enough, Hammond," Cather's voice boomed angrily. "Any man who'd be maverick enough to suggest that we leave a couple of sick women behind and push on so you and your friends can get to Sacramento one day sooner is a low-down, miserable so-and-so and that's you, by Jupiter! We aren't stirring a step away from here till all our womenfolk are able to travel. That's final, Mister Hammond, so you and your friends get out of here. And the sooner we're rid of the likes of you, the better off we'll be!"

That was the end of the discussion. Hammond and his companions started away, stopping as Hammond spotted Bill Raines and halted in front of him.

"If you can use a hundred bucks cash," Hammond said, "we can use a guide. You interested?"

Raines shook his head.

"Hundred and a quarter then," Hammond said curtly. "That's the highest we'll go, so you'll have to take it or leave it."

"I'm leaving it."

"All right," Hammond said. "The heck with it. Chances are we'll do just as well by ourselves."

"Sure," Bill said easily. "And save that hundred and a quarter to boot."

Hammond frowned and swung away, and his companions darted after him, overtook him and ranged themselves on either side of him. They pushed their way through the crowd, shouldering people out of the way.

"Hey!" a man yelled. "What do we do?"

"What d'you think we do?" Hammond retorted. "We're pushing on, that's what!"

There was a bit of whooping and a hurried, excited scrambling about. Heads turned and eyes watched interestedly as Hammond's followers scurried about, boosted their families up into their wagons and leaped up on the seats, ready to pull out the minute Hammond gave the signal. Raines had turned, too, and now, his thumbs hooked in his gunbelt, he was watching as the gold hunters poised themselves, reins gripped tightly in their left hands, and their right hands curled around the brake handles. Towards the rear of the crowd was a handful of women. Anna and Katey were among them, and somewhat behind them was Peggy Taylor. When Raines smiled, Anna waved in response and nudged her daughter.

"He is smiling at us, Katrina," she said out of the corner of her mouth. "See?"

"What, Mama? Oh, Mr. Raines!"

"Smile back at him!" Anna muttered.

When Katey seemed to hesitate, Anna pushed her forward; when Raines started towards them, Anna's arm shot out. She caught Katey by the arms and jerked her

38

to a stop.

"Wait," Anna commanded in a low voice. "He is coming."

Raines was within a dozen feet of the Heydrichs' when he swerved and suddenly halted.

"Peggy!" he called. And the Heydrichs' smiles vanished, their heads turned as one and their eyes focused on a slim girl who acknowledged Bill's call with an understanding nod, then backed out of the crowd and circled it. Anna and Katey saw her come up to Raines and smile up at him. Their lips seemed to tighten just the barest bit as Raines took her by the arm and led her away.

"That girl," Anna said presently. "You know who she is?"

"I think I've seen her before," Katey answered. "I don't know her name, though."

"I will find out who she is," Anna said. "Then we will meet her."

"What good will that do?"

Anna was herself again. She smiled deeply.

"You will see," she said. "Come. We must go back now. Papa will be wondering where we are."

A whip cracked suddenly with an explosive report and everyone stopped and looked up. A big wagon came lumbering forward. It was Hammond's. He was poised on the driver's seat with a long whip clutched in his right hand. Now other wagons pulled out of line—one, two, three, four, five, six, seven, eight! Slowly they swung in behind Hammond's wagon, forming a line of their own. Big wheels churned the dirt and dust began to rise. Bill Raines and Peggy Taylor had stopped to watch. Slowly the nine wagons trundled along the line of idling wagons;

presently Hammond's was clear of the Andersons' wagon and turning westward. The other wagons followed.

Will Cather had jumped down from the Andersons' wagon and stood stiffly in front of it, followed the departing wagons with angry eyes; after they had gone, he turned and faced the people who were standing around.

"Now look, you folks," he began, and men and women crowded around him. "If there's anybody else around here who figures he's losing dough by having to lay over for a couple of days, the thing for him to do is to harness up and get going while the going is still good. There's no law, y'know, that says you've got to stay put here if you don't want to."

No one moved.

Cather grunted.

"All right then," he continued. "Mrs. Archer, I'm told, is in a pretty bad way. Just how bad, I don't know. I'm no doctor, and I'm no midwife. I'm only a man. But you women, 'specially the ones who've had kids, you ought to be able to understand how sick a woman can be at a time like this, better than I can ever hope to tell you. So I'm not going to try. I think this lay-over is just about the best thing that could've happened to us. I mean it. I think we can all use a lay-off. I know danged well the horses can stand a rest, even if the rest of us don't think we need it. All right. You fellers who can't set down, give your wagons a look-over, tightening up and fixing whatever needs it. Then once we get rolling again, everything'll be just so and maybe we can really make time."

*　　*　　*

The day passed and finally it was evening.

There was no change in Mrs. Archer's condition; the

women did not expect any that soon and insisted there would not be any until morning. Some of them were certain it would be two or three days before anyone would really know. The men did not argue. There was no argument any of them could advance, and for once the word of the women was accepted as final.

Camp fires sprang up and lanterns gleamed all along the line of wagons, and soon the appetising aroma of cooking filled the air. Supper was barely over when night came on.

Bill Raines and Peggy Taylor had had an early supper. Now they were sitting in silence on the blanket-covered seat of Peggy's wagon. Bill's eyes ranged skywards and Peggy watched him; a couple of times he stood up and looked westward.

"What is it, Bill?" she asked finally.

"Huh? Oh, nothing."

There was another period of silence.

"You're unusually quiet tonight," Peggy remarked. "Are you worried about anything?"

"Just wondering how Hammond's bunch is doing," he replied. "They've got women and kids with them, y'know, and I'd sure hate to think of them running into something they might not be able to handle."

"Oh," Peggy said. "You mean like McBride?"

He nodded mutely.

"I thought you said McBride wouldn't dare come near us again."

"Hammond's outfit isn't part of ours any longer," Bill pointed out.

"Oh," Peggy said again.

He got to his feet, hitched up his pants and shifted his

gunbelt.

"Look," he said. "It's late and it's beginning to blow up. Suppose you turn in? I'm going over to see Cather."

"And then?"

"Y'mean after I see him?"

"Yes."

"Oh, I don't know. Maybe I'll just ride out a ways and have a look around."

She did not say anything further; she simply looked at him. When he gazed at her in turn, she turned her head. He put a big finger under her chin and turned her head around.

"If you're worrying that something's liable to happen to me, don't. I'm not looking for trouble, believe me."

"Well——" she said, and stopped.

"Well, what?"

"Nothing. Goodnight, Bill."

"Night," he said, but he did not move. Neither did she. Then he bent his head and kissed her gently on the lips. "You go to sleep. When I get back I'll curl up under here the same as I did last night. All right?"

"Hey," a voice called suddenly. "That you up there, Bill?"

Raines wheeled and looked down.

"Oh, hello, Will. I was just going to look you up. Anything the matter?"

Cather halted and leaned against the big wheel.

"Evening, Miss Taylor," he said. "Bill, I've been wondering if it mightn't be a good idea if one of us was to take a half dozen men and ride out a ways just to see that everything's all right. It's not that I've got any particular love for that Hammond feller or that I care a hoot

42

what happens to him. It's . . ."

"I know, Will. It's the women and kids with him."

"Right."

"I'll go," Raines said. "I can do with some exercise."

"You're sure you don't mind going? Miss Taylor, you don't . . ."

"She's turning in," Raines told him.

"Oh," Cather said. "Then it's all right. Bill, if you mosey down the line you'll find all the men you can use just hanging around and waiting for something to do."

Raines jumped down and strode away into the darkness.

"Bill!" Cather called.

"Yeah?"

"I'll wait up till you get back. I'll want to know if anything's happened. And one thing more."

"What?"

"Watch yourself, y'hear?"

CHAPTER IV

THE WANING night wind pushed against the tied-down canvas curtain and caused it to strain against its fastenings in the floor of the wagon. The leather tie-strings twisted and squeaked in the metal rings and produced an annoying creaking that finally startled Peggy Taylor into wakefulness; she sat upright and listened for a moment. She could hear nothing now save the stamp of horses's hooves; the wind had gone and the curtain hung stiffly as if it had been starched. She drew her blanket high, for it was chilly. Her first thought was of Bill Raines.

He had kissed her so gently, yet she fancied she could still feel the pressure of his lips against hers. She supposed she should have done something about the kiss. Why, she did not know, save that girls who were kissed, suddenly or otherwise, were supposed to react in some silly way, indignantly, she guessed, or perhaps they were supposed to appear offended, even hurt. But she had not felt that way at all. Perhaps she should have pushed him away, a warning to him that he was not to try it a second

44

time. She had not done anything. If he had attempted to kiss her a second time, she supposed he would have succeeded, and very likely she would not have done anything about that kiss either. She wondered if she had blushed. But she did not wonder about it very long, for she was quite certain that she had not. And if she had blushed, it was so dark he would not have noticed it. There had not been anything startling about the kiss, nothing very breathtaking, either. They had been standing very close together; actually there was not very much standing room in front of the driver's seat. It was dark, and when he bent over her she knew in that moment that he was going to kiss her—and he did.

Suddenly she wondered if he had returned. There was no reason for her to doubt it, yet something made her wonder.

She got to her feet, wrapped the blanket around her tightly, untied one end of the curtain-drop, pulled it back and peered out. It looked cold outside. Her eyes ranged upwards. The sky was drab and grey and empty. She wondered what time it was; she glanced skywards a second time and decided that it was about five o'clock. She climbed up on the seat, swung herself over it, eased herself down to the wheel, bent down and peered under the wagon. There was nothing under it. She straightened up. Awkwardly, because the blanket trailed between her legs and under her feet, she managed to get back inside the wagon. The curtain thumped into place.

It was some ten minutes later when it was whipped back and she reappeared. This time she was fully dressed. Now it was a comparatively simple matter for her to hoist herself up on the seat, swing herself over it, then climb down to the ground. She looked skywards again; there was a noticeable brightening in the sky. Soon it would be dawn. She turned and looked up the line to where the Andersons' wagon stood alone. She wondered if Cather was in there, asleep, or if he was up and around, waiting as he had promised for Bill to return.

"Good morning," she heard a voice say, and she turned around quickly.

A rather plump woman, blonde, blue-eyed and smiling, had just come around the wagon.

"Oh!" Peggy said. She looked a bit startled.

"I hope I did not frighten you."

"Only for the minute."

"I am Anna Heydrich," she said. "We are neighbours. We should know each other, no?"

"Yes, of course."

"Perhaps you know my daughter, Katrina?" Anna asked; then she laughed softly and shook her head. "She does not like it when I call her that. She says I must call her Katey. It is more American."

Peggy smiled.

"And my husband, Kurt? You do not know him either?"

"I'm afraid not, Mrs. Heydrich."

"Then I will introduce you. You will like them. Everybody does. 'Specially Katrina. She is so pretty. You should ask that tall young man—what is his name—oh, yes, Raines. Mr. Raines, I mean. He could not take his eyes off my Katrina."

Peggy offered no comment.

"It was the first time he had seen her," Anna went on, "and he looked—oh, how do you call it in English?"

46

"Enchanted?"

"Enchanted, yes," Anna said quickly. "When we lived in Illinois it was the same thing. Every young man there had eyes only for Katrina. The other girls did not like it a bit, but what can you do when a girl is so pretty? But enough about my Katrina for now. You are a nice-looking girl. Your colour, though, it is not very good. Perhaps you do not eat enough meat or drink enough milk, yes? What is your name?"

"Peggy, Mrs. Heydrich. Peggy Taylor."

"Peggy Taylor," Anna repeated. "Peggy Taylor. I like it. It is a very nice name."

"Thank you."

"Your family, they are already in California and now you go to join them there?"

"I haven't any family."

Anna looked shocked.

"Oh," she said. "I am sorry to hear about that. For a man to be alone—well, it is bad, but a man can manage. For a girl," Anna shook her head, "it is not good."

There was a moment's silence; it was Anna who broke it.

"What will you do when you get to California?" she asked.

"Work."

"Yes, but where?"

"Wherever I can get it."

"H'm," Anna said thoughtfully; then she smiled. "How would you like to live with us?"

"Why, I . . . "

"We will buy a farm and you could live with us. We are a very happy family, and you would be one of us. Of course I know you would not want to live with us for

47

nothing, so you could help me around the house. Not like a servant; like a daughter. You would have a home, a family, everything. You would like that, no?"

"You're awfully kind, Mrs. Heydrich, and I want you to know I appreciate it, but I . . ."

Anna's smile had gone; her eyes were icy cold.

"You are too good, maybe, for such work? It is not fancy enough for you?"

"I didn't say that."

"You think perhaps this Raines will marry you, and that then you will be a fine lady and you will not have to work at all?"

Peggy stiffened. She turned away, but Anna had not finished with her; she caught Peggy by the arm and spun her around.

"You think a man like him will marry you, a nobody, when there is my Katrina who has so much to offer him? You are fooling yourself, if that is what you think."

"Mrs Heydrich," Peggy said evenly "I don't think I like you. In fact, I know I don't. Now suppose you take your hand off my arm?"

Anna smiled coldly.

"I think I should tell you, Peggy Taylor, that I have decided that Mr. Raines will marry my daughter," she said. "I will not like it if you should interfere. Because I want we should be friends, I am warning you. So if you are a smart girl, you will not encourage Mr. Raines in his attentions to you. Now we understand each other, no, Peggy?"

Peggy pulled away She whirled around. then stopped abruptly as a tall figure appeared before her. She raised her eyes to meet Raines'.

"Well, well, the lucky man!" she cried.

Raines looked sharply at her, shifted his eyes momentarily to Anna Heydrich, then back to Peggy.

"It certainly isn't every man who can be so lucky," Peggy went on sarcastically. "It isn't every man who can acquire two charming women like Mama Heydrich and her beautiful daughter just by marrying the daughter. You're to be congratulated, Mr. Raines. I hope you'll be very, very happy."

Bill frowned. He pushed his hat back from his eyes and hooked his thumbs in his gunbelt.

"Wait a minute," he said curtly.

"You're angry, aren't you?" Peggy asked. She shook her head sadly. "You didn't want me to know, did you? Oh, I'm so sorry, Bill. I should have pretended I didn't know anything about your romance with the beautiful Katrina—I mean Katey. But Mama Heydrich didn't tell me I wasn't supposed to know. But don't feel too badly, Bill. Mama and Katey will make it up to you. Mama particularly. You'll be surprised at the things she can do; that is, when you really get to know her."

"Let me know when you get finished," Raines said.

"I'm finished now!" Peggy cried. "I never want to see you again!"

She flashed past him, climbed swiftly into the wagon, and the canvas curtain thumped down behind her.

It was evening when Peggy emerged from her wagon. The air was brisk and cool and the sky was blue and starry. She heard a boot crunch shale and pebbles and she looked away quickly.

"Peggy," she heard Raines say.

She did not answer.

49

"Peggy," he said a second time.

"Go away."

"You have any supper?"

"I don't want any."

"Climb down here," he commanded. "Come on."

"No."

"Do I have to come up there and get you?"

There was no reply, and no movement on Peggy's part.

"Look," Raines said quietly. "I haven't got time for playing tonight. McBride's outfit shot up Hammond's bunch and we're liable to get it tonight. I arranged for you to move in with Mrs. Anderson. It'll be better that way all around, safer, and it'll mean company for you too, specially at night when Cather and Anderson and me are on the go. Mrs. Anderson's got some supper ready for you, so we don't want to keep her waiting. Besides, I've got things to do. So come on. Climb down here."

She turned slowly, finally raised her eyes to his.

"Well——" she began.

"Come on."

She got to her feet.

"The women and children with Hammond," she said. "Were they all right when you found them?"

"Some of them," he replied. "Hammond's wife was among the ones killed. Seven of their nine wagons are gone, burned to the ground. We brought back the other two."

She eased herself over the wheel and he held up his arms. His big hands caught her. He lifted her and set her down gently on the ground. She avoided his eyes, smoothed her dress down to avoid looking up at him. He took her arm and led her up the line to the Andersons' wagon.

"Oh," she said when they stopped in front of it. "I wonder if Mrs. Archer is feeling better. Have you heard anything?"

"Y'mean you haven't?"

"Why no, Bill."

"She's dead," he said grimly. "We buried her at noon."

Her hand tightened on his arm.

"Bill!" she said in a shocked voice.

"Her troubles are over," he added. "Look. I can't stand here all night, so I'll make it short. When I decide to get married, I'll be the one to tell you about it. I won't leave it to somebody else to do. That clear? Next, that Katrina or Katey or whatever the heck her name is—she's a nice-looking girl. That don't mean I'm going to marry her, even if her Ma does think it'd be a swell idea. I've got some ideas of my own and they don't include the Heydrichs. Now the girl I marry is going to be smart and calm and she's not going to be the kind who acts up like a kid who's still wet behind the ears. You might remember that if you expect me to marry you."

"And what makes you think I want you to?"

The grimness in his face vanished; he grinned down at her.

"You," he said calmly. He bent his head and kissed the tip of her nose. "Come on. Up you go."

He lifted her lightly. She caught the rim of the seat and pulled herself up, turned and looked down at him.

"See you in the morning," he said as he turned away.

"Bill," she called.

He stopped, looked at her over his shoulder, then came striding back.

"Yeah?"

"Bill, I'm awfully sorry I acted the way I did. It was childish and I'm sorry. But it won't happen again. That's a promise."

He reached up and patted her hand.

"Forget it," he said. "Night."

"Good night, Bill."

*　　*　　*

It was midnight and the train was shrouded in darkness and slumbering silence. Even the usually restless horses huddled together peacefully. A wind raced over the range, rustled the grass, whipped some dust about. The canvas top of one of the darkened wagons creaked a bit when the wind surged against it; then after a minute everything grew quiet again.

Fifty feet away from the Anderson wagon a man lay on his stomach in the grass. He raised himself once and looked northwards when he thought he heard something; after a while he relaxed, turned over on his back and lay flat, looking up at the sky. Presently he rolled over on his stomach, got up on his knees, picked up his rifle and came erect to his feet. He looked towards the long double row of darkened wagons and shook his head.

"Damn foolishness, I call it," he muttered. "Nobody in his right mind's going to attack an outfit the size of this one. I wish to blazes Cather or one of the others was out here instead of me. I'm so blamed tired and sleepy, I'm jiggered if I know what's keeping my eyes open. Could I do a job of sleeping! Bet I wouldn't wake up for a week if I got the chance, 'specially right now."

He was stiffly silent for a moment, considering. Then he trudged away, marched past the Anderson wagon, past a

52

couple more, stopped finally in front of a huge prairie schooner, looked around quickly, got down on his knees and crawled in between the big wheels.

"The heck with it," he muttered. "I'm sleepy and that's that. I'm no soldier. If they want guards, let them hire some. Me, I'm going to get some sleep, and anybody who don't like it don't have to."

He stretched out on his back with his rifle beside him, sighed deeply, wearily. After a minute he rolled over on his side, and a minute later he was asleep. A wind droned over the range and swept dust and leaves over him, but he did not move.

Fifty feet northwards of his post, shadowy figures crawled over the ground, stopping every few minutes to look up. Four shadows came closer and revealed themselves to be four men. They crept past the very spot on which he had been sprawled out earlier, inched their way forward within a dozen feet of it. One of the men turned and made a beckoning motion, and his companions joined him. There was a minute-long whispered conversation; then the four men arose and rushed headlong towards the wagons directly ahead of them. They came skidding up to them, dropped down and pushed their way in between the wheels, huddled behind them. There was a strange scratching sound then flame suddenly spurted out beneath the wagons and the men, each of them gripping a couple of lighted faggots in his hands, came scrambling out. They had already chosen the wagons they would attack; accordingly they separated, and dashed away. A flaming brand was hurled atop one wagon and the heat-dried canvas covering instantly ignited. Another wagon was similarly attacked, but the firebrand slid off the canvas top and dropped on the driver's seat, where it sputtered noisily for a moment. Then flames ringed the seat and hungry fingers of fire reached out, some towards the wheels and the shaft, while others raced up the length of the canvas curtain, spanned it and reached the top of the wagon and bit into it with a hissing sound that became an ominous crackling. Sparks from burning wagons leaped into the air and the wind caught them up, whipped through space and dropped on to still other wagons. Flames broke out in a dozen places along the line. There was a scream, a cry, a yell, followed by a rush of booted feet.

"Come on!" a voice hollered.

Shadowy figures wheeled away from the burning wagons and darted off into the darkness. A rifle cracked and one of the running men stumbled and fell on his hands and knees. He forced himself up again, and was staggering away when the rifle thundered a second time. The man stopped, stiffened and pitched forward on his face in the grass. There was a clatter of hooves, and a handful of horsemen, six or eight of them, came whirling down the line, swerved and dashed through a dark space between two wagons; then, fanning out, they pounded away in pursuit of the faggot throwers.

"Don't let a one of them get away!" a voice yelled.

In the darkness beyond the wagons a gun roared spitefully and a man cried out. Other guns joined in, adding their voices to the mounting din of screams and crackling fires. A man seeking to escape a pursuing horseman came running back towards the wagons, twisted around and fired. A rifle-armed man peered out at him from between the spokes of a big wheel, raised the rifle to his shoulder, poking the barrel between the spokes, aimed and pulled the trigger. The man with the six-gun in his hand stumbled awkwardly and nearly fell, braced himself on failing legs, steadied himself and slowly raised his gun. The rifle and the six-gun roared simultaneously, the two shots blending into one. The six-gun slid out of the man's numbed hand and dropped into the grass. He fell limply to the ground. The rifle man dropped his weapon. He sagged brokenly against the wheel, crumpled up and fell backwards into the shadows beneath the big wagon.

The train was fully awake now. Men ran this way and that. Some leaped up on the burning wagons and tore the canvas away, while others dashed up and helped frightened people to the ground. Horses milled about, whinnying to be untied from the burning wagons. Knives flashed in the moonlight and cut into tethering ropes and the horses, released, wheeled and galloped away.

* * *

When the dawn sun rose, the smouldering embers of fourteen wagons offered mute testimony to the effectiveness of the attack. Groups of white-faced, tired-looking people stood around here and there, and there was little or no conversation among them. They were too worn out, now that the shock of the attack had passed, to do anything but stand around listlessly, even though many of them seemed to have little energy left for any purpose. When they moved they were heavy-footed and apparently aimless. Twenty-one motionless, blanket-covered bodies lay on the ground between the rows of wagons. Heavy-lidded eyes stared at them and stunned heads bowed and shook. Tiny children, some of them not fully dressed, and many of them hollow-eyed and still showing signs of frenzied fright, wandered about, too. Each time one of them came up to the dead bodies, the child would stop and stare at the corpses, circle them and go on quickly, only to stop and look back, gasp and wheel and run.

Peggy Taylor was standing in front of the Anderson wagon when Bill Raines sauntered up.

"Hello," he said. He leaned against the big wheel, eased his hat up from his eyes. His face was drawn and streaked and his hands were dirty.

"Can I get you anything, Bill? Some coffee?"

He shook his head.

"No, thanks. I've had more than my share of coffee already."

She moved a bit closer to him.

"Bill, McBride will be back again, won't he?" she asked.

"Till he gets what he wants."

Her eyes ranged past him for a moment, over the groups of people beyond them.

"Y'see, Peg," he went on, "this is one of the biggest trains that ever set out for California; leastways, it was in the beginning when we had a hundred and thirty-nine wagons and rigs. Up to now we've lost twenty-seven and there's maybe eight or ten just about ready to fall apart the minute we hit rough country. But getting back to McBride, he's figured out that a train this size must be carrying a lot of dough. Know what Cather's strongbox has got in it?"

She turned to him again, and shook her head.

"Eighty-six thousand dollars," he said. "Cash."

She smiled fleetingly.

"Two hundred of it is mine."

"None of it's mine. Anyway, you know what McBride's

after. All we can do is fight him off the best way we can. 'Course we know he'll jump us every chance he gets, so we've got to be ready for him every minute of the day and night. There'll be burning and killing every mile of the way into California. It'll be a blood trail all the way and we'll be sweating blood every inch of it."

"Will we be here much longer?"

He shook his head.

" We're pulling out of here at noon. Fix yourself something to eat early, so you'll be set to leave the minute Cather gives the word."

CHAPTER V

AT NOON, with a seering sun overhead, the train stirred
itself into movement. Whips cracked all along the length
of the train. The horses dug their hooves into the ground;
wheels bit deep into the grass and dirt, creaked and
crunched—and big, top-heavy prairie schooners lurched
forward. As before, the train was drawn up in a double
line with probably a dozen feet of sunlit space between
the two lines. Twenty rifle-armed horsemen rode on the
flanks of the train to guard against a sudden swooping
raid, although no one, not even Cather, expected McBride
to attempt an attack in broad daylight. But everyone
seemed so uneasy, once the train got under way, that
Cather quickly organised a crew of outriders and sent
them loping away with instructions to shoot without a
moment's delay if anything unusual or even questionable
occurred. As the train started off, the women and children in the party hurried to the rear of their respective
wagons for a last look at the hastily cleared cemetery in
which the twenty-one victims of McBride's wanton attack

had been laid to rest but an hour before. There was a single grave somewhat apart from the others which was Sarah Archer's resting place. Tear-filled eyes did not turn away until the cemetery had disappeared from view, lost in the heat haze, the rising dust, and the distance.

Cather and Raines rode at the head of the train; a couple of hundred yards ahead of them rode two scouts. Every once in a while either Cather or Raines would swing around and ride back the full length of the train just to see that everything was all right; after a while, usually some fifteen or twenty minutes later, the other would wheel away and lope back.

"McBride must have added to his outfit to get up enough nerve to tackle us," Cather remarked after a brief spell of thoughtful silence.

"Sure looks like it."

"Funny, isn't it," Cather mused, "how a bad man can always find company or know where to go to find it?"

"Word gets around," Raines said, "and as soon as a bad man has to hit the trail he knows where to go to find some of his own kind. You ever see any of those little one-horse towns in the hill country?"

"Nope."

"You haven't missed anything then, believe me. They're not actually towns. Usually they're nothing more than a handful of dirty shacks and maybe a saloon, and that's all. Just a holing-up spot for outlaws trying to keep a step ahead of the law and a hanging. Most of the time every last man in those towns is high-tailing it from the law, so when another feller riding hell-bent for election shows up, nobody asks him any questions. Everybody can tell by looking at him that he's one of them, and nobody bothers him."

"How come the law don't do something about them? Seems to me they'd at least give it a try."

"That sounds a heap easier to do than it is," Raines answered. "You'd need a whole regiment of cavalry to do it, and where d'you suppose you'd get the regiment? Usually those towns are set on high ground with a commanding view of the countryside for miles around. You can figure out for yourself what a job it'd be for any outfit, 'specially a posse with its dozen or fifteen men, to try to attack a place like that. They wouldn't stand a chance. A couple of good shots with rifles shooting down into them while they were having their own troubles riding uphill in rough country—cripes, you wouldn't need more than a couple of men to hold off a couple of hundred. That's where outfits like McBride's are recruited."

"H'm," Cather said. "Well, we'll have to keep our eyes peeled for them all the time."

"And our rifles loaded and handy, too."

There was no further conversation for a few minutes; then Raines wheeled his horse alongside Cather's.

"Will, how far d'you figure to go today?" the younger man asked.

Cather smiled grimly.

"Just as far as we can," he answered. "If it wasn't for the women and the kids, I'd keep pushing ahead straight through, clear up to daylight. If McBride took it into his head to attack us when we were on the move, he wouldn't find the going easy, not with every man in the train awake and ready for him. His only chance is to swoop down on us when we've pulled up for the night and we're asleep. But if we could drive by night and lay up in the daytime, he'd have one helluva party. He'd be lucky to get away alive."

"You might have something there, y'know?"

Cather grunted.

"If that hellion pushes us too far," he said with grim finality, "I'll be tempted to try it."

"Why wait for him to give us another dose of fire? We've had a sample of it already, and the twenty-one we left behind us . . . "

"Don't go getting ahead of yourself, Bill. Let's kinda wait and see what happens."

Raines' shoulders lifted in an empty shrug.

"You're the boss," he said, "and you make the decisions. Only I hope you don't wait too long to do it."

He loped away again.

He glanced at the three people who were riding on the wide seat of the Anderson wagon as he neared it. Anderson was driving. Peggy Taylor sat next to him and Mrs. Anderson flanked her on the other side. Peggy gave him a warm smile as he came loping abreast of them. He winked back at her. He saw a smile cross Mrs. Anderson's face, and he saw her lips move as she said something to Peggy, who blushed and hurriedly averted her eyes. Raines rode on. Katey and Anna were riding together as usual in the first of the Heydrich wagons. Both lifted their eyes to Raines as he came along and both smiled at him, Katey fleetingly and a bit shyly, Anna with her purposeful, deepening and dimpling smile. Raines touched his hat to them as he rode by. Kurt Heydrich, alone and massive as he sat hunched over the reins in the second wagon, nodded to him and Bill responded with a nod.

"Young feller!" Kurt called, and Raines pulled up,

wheeled around and rode back.

"Yeah? You call me, Mr. Heydrich?"

"How far do we go today?"

Raines smiled.

"As far as we can," he replied.

Kurt nodded approvingly.

"Good," he said. "Good. Maybe then we can make up some time, no?"

"That's the general idea," Bill said and rode off.

Minutes later he ranged up alongside of Cather.

"Yeah?" the latter asked. "Everything all right?"

Raines eased himself in the saddle.

"So far," he said.

An hour passed, two, three, all of them slowly and uneventfully. The turning wheels rumbled steadily westward. The wearied horses plodded on head-bowed. Five o'clock came and went and still Cather pushed on. The sun eased off towards six, slipped away to the west, and thin, timid shadows began to appear. The line of outriders on the northern side of the train wavered and bent in the middle as some of the horsemen moved in closer to the train, looking in Cather's direction, and wondering when he intended to stop. He gave no indication that he noticed them. He rode on doggedly, grimly, too, his eyes holding steadily on the range that spread away before him. Slowly the line of horsemen drifted back and it straightened out again and the train moved on as before.

But after a while, when the shadows began to lengthen and deepen, and dusk came on, Cather jerked his mount to a halt. Raines pulled up too.

"All right, Bill," Cather said to him. "Reckon we've covered enough ground for today."

Raines swung away from him and rode back to meet the oncoming wagons.

"Pull up!" he yelled through cupped hands. "Pull up!"

The wagons ground to a stop. Handbrakes rasped and squeaked as they were yanked back. Wearied horses standing on wide-spread, quivering legs, breathed loudly and blew themselves. Raines looked back when he heard the lifting beat of hooves somewhere in the distance beyond him. He saw the two scouts ride up to Cather and flank him. He squared around again and rode on.

"Don't crowd the other feller," he called to one wagon driver. He wanted to add: "Fire can spread like all getout once it gets started," but he held his tongue.

There was a sizable gap between two wagons and he wheeled through it and outside the train on to the range itself. An outrider looked at him hopefully.

"We're making camp here for tonight," Raines called to him.

The man whipped off his hat, waved it and hollered. The other horsemen came racing towards the train as swiftly as their tired horses could negotiate the distance. Raines turned his mount and rode back to where Cather had stopped. He nodded to the scouts when they trudged past him leading their horses.

"Might be a good idea," he said to Cather, "to string out another bunch of riflemen tonight. They could bust up a sneak attack even before it got started. That all right with you?"

"Yeah, sure," the older man said quickly. "I'm for anything that'll save lives."

"Got another idea, too," Raines said with a grin. "How would it be if we were to start a whole circle of fires, sort of ring the train with them, say about a hundred feet away from the train and with the fires about forty or fifty feet apart? We could keep them burning full blast all night long, and if any of McBride's mavericks tried to come through, it'd be like shooting at a standing target to knock them off. How's it sound to you? All right?"

"Sounds like you're expecting company tonight," Will Cather said.

"And how I'm expecting it," Raines said calmly. "But I won't be the least bit disappointed if nobody shows up."

Cather looked at him for a moment.

"You get any more bright ideas," he said, "and I'll be looking for a new job. What are you trying to do—show up the old man?"

"Huh?" Raines asked innocently. "What d'you mean . . . show you up? You don't realise it, partner, but it's little things that you say from time to time that gives me ideas, so you're just as much responsible for them as I am. That showing you up?"

Cather laughed.

"Go on," he said. "Don't try to pull the wool over my eyes."

"On the level, Will."

"You're the blamedest, doggonedest liar and you know it," Cather insisted.

"Could be," the youth said easily, quite unworried. "But if you keep it to yourself, nobody else will ever know it."

"Go on," Cather said again. "Go get yourself some grub, you fresh young pup, and don't try to fool the old man again. Y'hear?"

"Nope," Raines said with a grin. "And if anybody asks me how come the fires or the outriders, I'm going to tell them it was all your idea."

He wheeled his mount and rode away.

* * *

Riflemen—only this time they were dismounted and ordered to squat in the shadows out of range of the crackling fires that ringed the train—took up their posts under Bill Raines' eye. The fires themselves were started on stony ground, and as an added precaution to prevent the flames from feasting on and spreading over the sun-dried grass, rocks and stones were heaped around the base of each fire, thus confining it to the immediate vicinity. The only fear, therefore, was of a strong wind, but fortunately, while it was cool, even chilly, the wind was negligible and few sparks were wafted away from the fires. At the Andersons' insistence. Will Cather rolled himself up in his blankets in Peggy's wagon, and fifteen minutes after, when John Anderson peered in on him, he found Cather fast asleep and "snoring like a good feller." Raines did not turn in. He insisted he could not and added, when Peggy looked at him, that he would sleep all the next day. Peggy shook her head, but he chucked her under the chin, tossed her a cheery "good night" and went off.

"You're going to marry him, aren't you?" Mrs. Anderson asked when they were alone behind the canvas drop.

Peggy did not answer as promptly as she should have, and Mrs. Anderson smiled understandingly.

"You don't have to answer," she said. "You two were meant for each other. Anyone can see that. It's in your eyes, and in his, the way you look at each other."

Peggy smiled a little, and blushed a little.

"He's asked you, of course, hasn't he?"

"Well, not exactly."

Mary Anderson's eyes widened.

"Oh," she said. "I'm sorry, Peggy. I . . ."

"I meant," Peggy said quickly, "that while he hasn't actually asked me, he's told me."

"Told you?" Mrs. Anderson repeated; then she laughed softly. "Oh, I see! But I suppose that that's the way of the modern generation. Imagine a young man telling a young woman in my time that he was going to marry her and considering the subject closed and final. Our mothers would have had a fit!"

Peggy smiled again.

"I'm sure it would have been different with us if conditions had been different," she explained. "Riding in a wagon doesn't exactly lead to romance, you know, particularly with so many people watching you all the time and so many things happening all around you. Then, too, Bill's had to be on the go all the time, or nearly all the time, doing his work as Mr. Cather's assistant. So you mustn't think badly of him."

Mrs. Anderson patted Peggy's hand.

"I don't at all," she said quickly. "In view of conditions, I think he's done wonderfully well. And now that I think of things, it's a wonder to me that you two had any time together at all."

"We didn't have very much," Peggy admitted. "It was mostly at supper-time or for just a little while after supper that we got a chance to talk, and what little we know about each other . . . "

There was a sudden thumping on the floor of the wagon, and Peggy stopped abruptly and looked at Mrs. Anderson.

"Hey," a muffled voice said from under the wagon, "how d'you expect a feller to sleep with all that jawing going on, huh?"

"It's John," Mary Anderson said. "We'd better get to bed. Ready?"

Peggy got under the blanket.

"Ready," she said.

Mrs. Anderson blew out the light. She groped her way in the darkness to Peggy's side, climbed in beside her, and settled herself with a sigh. There was no further conversation. They were tired, and presently their gentle breathing indicated that they were asleep.

＊　＊　＊

It was shortly after midnight when Bill Raines came trudging through the grass midway between the darkened wagons and the line of riflemen.

"Looks like we all could've turned in," a voice said from the shadows nearby. "That McBride's not going to come messing around here tonight."

Raines halted.

"How d'you know?" he asked.

"Oh, if he was coming, he would've been here by now," the man insisted.

"Y'mean he only works certain hours, or have you and him got it arranged when he can pull off a raid and when he can't?"

"That supposed to be funny?"

"It's not supposed to be anything. I'm only asking a question."

"Look, Mister," the man said, "I'm not here to take any sass from you or anybody else. That clear?"

"Yeah, sure."

"All right then. How'd you like to take over for me, huh? You don't give a hang if you sleep or not. Me, I like to sleep when it comes night. How about it?"

"You got a family in the train?" Raines asked.

"Sure, but what's that got to do with it?"

"Just this. Long as we've got women and kids to take care of, we've got to do everything we can to protect them. Standing guard at night in order to prevent McBride from pulling off another sneak raid and killing off some more of our people is one of the things we have to do. That too much for you to understand?"

"Look, Mister . . ."

"I'm looking," Bill said curtly. "If standing guard to protect your own family is asking too much of you, you go ahead and turn in. Chances are you wouldn't be a bit of good around here if a raid was pulled off, anyway. Go ahead. We can get along without you."

"Why, you . . . "

"Yeah?" the tall youth taunted him.

"Long as I'm out here, I'll stay put, but the first thing tomorrow morning I'm going to hunt you up, and when I catch up with you, I'm going to give you the damnedest walloping anybody ever got."

"I can hardly wait," Raines said. "Oh, yeah, just in case you forget or get cold feet, and I have to go hunt you up, where'll I find you?"

The man laughed. His climbed to his feet and stretched himself. He was a big fellow. In the distorting night light he was huge.

"Just ask anybody in the train for Tom Howell," he answered lightly. "Everybody knows me. They'll be able to tell you where I'm at."

"Right," Raines said, and he strode away.

There was no attack, not even a sign of McBride or of

his men, and the uneventful night, long and wearying, seemed unending. The fires died out just before dawn and no one did anything to rekindle them. The guards, relaxing, climbed stiffly to their feet, stamped on the ground, yawned and stretched and looked skywards. Empty, colourless and drab one minute, the next minute the sky was filled with awakening light. The shadows of night lifted and vanished into thin air, and then it was day. Tom Howell was hitching up his pants when he heard an approaching footstep. He turned, looked hard and grunted.

"Oh," he said. "So it's you, eh?"

"Yeah," Raines said. "In the flesh."

Howell grunted again.

"This spot suit you all right?" he asked.

"Good as any other, I suppose."

Howell gave him a curious look, took off his hat and scaled it away. He unbuckled his gunbelt, wound the belt around the holstered gun and put it down in the grass. He unbuttoned his shirt and took it off and tossed it aside, hitched up his pants again and looked up.

"All right," he said. "Come and get it."

Raines smiled fleetingly.

"Sure," he said. "Anything to oblige."

Howell, his big fists clenched and raised, came plunging across the grass. Raines side-stepped nimbly and Howell's swinging right fist missed him completely. Bill turned to meet the big man's second rush. It came without a moment's loss of time. This time Raines did not side-step at once. He waited until Howell was almost upon him; then he twisted away, ducked under a second wild swing, and came up suddenly with a short-arm jolt that landed squarely in the pit of Howell's stomach. Howell grunted and dropped his hands, and Raines promptly struck him in the face, and just as promptly moved away again.

Howell came lunging after him. Raines, whipping around, drove a long, lightning-like left into the man's face, brought up his right fist with an echoing thud, and when he stepped back again there was a crimson smear on Howell's lips and blood bubbles in his nostrils. Howell moved towards him again. He was breathing through his open mouth. He plunged across the intervening space, swung a big fist wildly, missed by a wide margin, and took a hard, full-bodied punch in return. It made him gasp, and he stumbled and fell on his hands and knees. Raines suddenly became aware of a circle of spectators. He made no attempt to force the fighting; he backed a bit, his hands lowered, and waited. Howell dragged himself up. Slowly he advanced, with his guard high to protect his battered face. Cautiously he thrust out his left. Raines brushed it aside and in almost the same motion drove his own left fist wrist-deep into Howell's stomach. Howell's mouth popped open and he gasped painfully. With one thick arm folded over his stomach and sucking in air through his open mouth, he began to retreat. Raines followed him doggedly, motioning to him to stand and fight. Hunching over a bit Howell pawed at him with his right. A long stabbing left to Howell's head snapped it back. Unconsciously his guard came up, leaving his stomach unprotected. Raines took prompt advantage of it and sank a hard right into his opponent's stomach, driving the breath out of him. He went down to his knees and fell forward on his hands.

Suddenly there was a yell from somewhere along the length of the train and the bystanders looked up. Raines backed away from his hunched-over opponent and raised his eyes in the direction from which the yell had come. There was another yell, a more frenzied one this time, and the sudden crack of a rifle. The last wagon in line was burning. Then the wagon directly ahead of it burst into flames. A third wagon, a fourth and then a fifth, all in the same line and one in front of the other ranging forward from the last one, began to burn. The entire train awoke. Men came leaping out of wagons all along the line. Women and children appeared too, and in another moment the train was in a uproar. Children were knocked down and trampled. Screaming, hysterical women clawed at men who bumped into them, and excited, running men collided full tilt with other men. Punches were thrown wildly in the confusion.

Raines bolted away. He remembered seeing Howell get to his feet and turn after him. But dashing off he was soon swallowed up by the panicking, milling crowd, and forgot about Howell. Panting up to the nearest burning wagon, Raines burst through the wide-eyed onlookers, leaped up on the driver's seat, ripped off the flame-ringed drop-curtain and flung it away. He reached up, got a grip on the canvas top and jerked at it furiously. It came away after a bit of a struggle and, twisting around, he sent it hurtling to the ground. A couple of men jumped on it and began to stamp out the flames

"Hey, Raines!" a man yelled. "Anybody in there?"

Raines shook his head.

"What'd you say?" the same man yelled.

The smoke filled Raines' throat and burned his eyes.

71

"Nobody in here," he managed to answer choked.

The man darted off. Raines climbed over the wheel and made his way down to the ground. The framework of the wagon was flame-ringed and fire was gnawing at it hungrily, loudly too, with a sort of swooshing sound. There was nothing that anyone could do about it, hence the onlookers, accepting the burning wagon as lost, moved away. The biggest crowd was gathered around the next wagon.

"This one's a goner too," a man said to Raines as he pushed through to it. "Wish I'd got the skunk who set it on fire. I got one shot at him, but he was moving too fast for me to hit him. Fact is I never saw anybody flit around the way he did. More like a shadow than a man."

"Who's this wagon belong to?"

"Tom Howell."

"O-h, yeah? Tom Howell, huh? Say, what about his family? They get out all right?"

"Yeah, sure," the man answered. "Only now that I think of it, it seems to me I saw Tom climbing back up here, only I don't think I saw him again after that. All the excitement, y'know. People stampin' around, women getting panicky and kids hollering." He turned to the people nearest him. "Any of you folks see Tom Howell?"

There was no answer. The flames from the burning wagon reached out hungrily and the people who had converged upon it hastily crowded back from it. The framework that supported the rounded top splintered and fell in on one side. A woman screamed and pointed hysterically.

"Look!" and she pointed. "A hand!"

Others also pointed to a hand that came creeping out of

the folds of burning canvas along the edge of the wagon's wooden wall; then the hand was withdrawn. Raines pushed the man out of his way, leaped up on the wheel, yanked off the curtain that hung in smoking tatters, tossed it to the ground; then he eased himself over the wide seat and dropped off it into the burning interior of the wagon. A couple of other men jumped up on the wagon. One of them climbed up on the seat, and bent down as if he were helping lift something. Another man jumped down, turned and held up his hands.

"All right!" he yelled. "Let me have him!"

Some men among the onlookers joined them. There was some straining just behind the seat, some laboured shoving and lifting, then a pair of booted feet came into view and a woman in the crowd gasped aloud. Now a body was being slid over the seat, and big hands reached it, got hold of it, cradled it in strong arms and backed away with it. A path opened before the men and they carried their burden to a grassy stretch of ground and laid it down. The men in the wagon climbed down. Raines, dirty-faced, made his way down to the ground just as the remaining side of the framework fell in. Sparks leaped high into the air, sprung around for a moment and then dropped earthwards. Men and children jumped for them, stamped them out. Raines stumbled away, sank down on the ground and sprawled out on his back. He closed his smarting eyes.

"Hey!" a man yelled. "He isn't dead! He's alive!"

There were more excited yells and everyone gathered around the figure stretched out on the grass. Raines forced himself up into a sitting position. A man came running past him, skidded to a stop in the grass, retraced his steps to Raines' side, bent over and peered hard at him.

"Hey, you all right?"

Raines' eyes were still smarting. But he opened them and struggled up into a sitting position. His eyes began to tear. They ran down his dirt-streaked cheeks. When he turned to wipe them away, he smudged his face even more.

"Yeah, I'm all right," he finally answered. He blinked at the man. "How's Howell? He making it all right?"

"Coming around fine," the man told him and straightened up. "Got himself a belly full of smoke. Aside from that, he's doing fine. And by morning he'll be as good as new."

The man stepped back and ran on.

CHAPTER VI

THE NEXT DAY was merely a carry-over of the previous night's misfortune. At mid-morning when the train got under way again, thin wisps of smoke were still rising from the burned-out hulks of the five wagons. By noon seven more wagons had to be emptied of their contents and abandoned. Broken axles, broken beyond repair, broken spoked wheels that could not be replaced, and crumbling wagon bodies that made further use of them dangerous, made abandonment necessary. Three o'clock saw two more wagons evacuated of their contents and occupants and left behind, and at sundown when the train ground to a halt, a tally of the wagons drawn up in the usual double line totalled eighty-one in all.

Cather shook his head sadly.

"Eighty-one left out of a hundred an' thirty-nine," he said to Raines when they were standing together at the head of the train looking down its length. Camp fires had already been lighted and were burning evenly. They could see little groups of people, children as well as grown-ups, gathered around the fires waiting for their supper to take edible form. "Eighty-one from a hundred an' thirty-nine leaves fifty-eight. That's how many we've lost so

75

far."

"I know," Raines answered. "And the rub is we're still a long, long way from California."

"That's what's bothering me," Cather said with another unhappy shake of his head. "I wish we were there already so everyone could go his own way and on his own, and I wouldn't have to worry about what might happen to them tonight and maybe another hundred nights still to come."

"What's happened and what's liable to happen can't be held against you," Raines insisted.

Cather did not agree with him.

"That's where you're wrong, Bill," he said. "For what's happened and for what's liable to happen, since I'm the one running the train, I'm the one who'll be held responsible. And don't you think for a minute, Bill, that there aren't those who are blaming me already. For what I didn't do and should have, leastways the way they have things figured, and for what I did and shouldn't have. And don't try to tell me different. I've been around a long time and I've met a lot of people in that time, and I know how they think. Because I know that, the whole thing is beginning to get me down."

"Will, you didn't go 'round holding a gun to the heads of these people, did you, and make them sign up for this trip with you? They did it of their own free will. Right? They must've known what lay ahead of them and what the chances were for everyone's getting through to California. So they must've been willing to take the chance. The ones who make it will have to agree they were lucky, and those who don't make it, we-ll, they were plain unlucky. It's that simple. So as I said before, what's happened and what's liable to happen can't be held against you."

"Bill, make it your business to notice the expression on the faces of those who've lost some of their folks, and you'll see right off how they feel about me. And it isn't kindly, believe me. You watch them when we pass them or when they come past us."

Cather lifted his eyes skywards. When Raines suddenly clamped his hand on Cather's arm, the older man looked at him questioningly.

"What d'you make of this, Will?" Raines asked and Cather ranged his gaze after the youth's pointing finger.

A tight little band of men was marching up the line to where Cather and Raines were standing.

"That's Hammond leading them, isn't it?" Cather asked, levelling a long, narrow-eyed look at the lanky man striding at the head of the oncoming group.

"Uh-huh," Raines said. "And something tells me you're going to have even more trouble on your hands. Those men look sore about something."

Cather frowned and spat in the grass.

"Their kind of trouble I can handle," he said. He hitched up his pants. "Let them come."

Hammond and those with him, eleven in all Raines counted, came striding up shortly. Hammond halted in front of Cather, a step ahead of the others who formed a half-circle around him.

"Well?" Cather demanded. "What kind of trouble have you stirred up this time, *Mister* Hammond?"

The lanky man flushed.

"I'm here because the men have asked me to do their talking for them," he replied, drawing himself up to his full height. His Adam's apple jerked and his jaw muscles twitched.

"All right," Cather said briskly. "I'm listening. Go ahead and talk."

Hammond cleared his throat.

"The men seem to think we might do better if we had someone else in charge of the train," he began.

Cather smiled thinly.

"You mean with you in charge, don't you?"

"I'm only telling you what the men asked me to say for them," Hammond replied a bit stiffly.

"All right, you've said it. So what?"

"I think they have a right to their opinion."

"Every man has a right to his opinion. Even you, Hammond. Even though you're a trouble-maker."

"Wait a minute now," another man said and he stepped up next to Hammond. "Look, Will. It isn't that we haven't got all the faith in the world in you."

"Oh, sure," Cather said.

"It's just that we think that maybe with someone else running things . . . "

"Like Hammond for instance?"

"Gimme a chance, will yuh, Will, to say what I want to say?"

"Wait a minute, Fuller," Cather commanded. "You're forgetting something. You people came to me and asked to join the train I was getting together to go to California. You even signed contracts with me. Right? You people own your own wagons, sure. But the train itself that consists of your wagons and everyone else's is mine. You signed with me, paid me what I asked for the privilege of joining my train, and I in turn contracted to lead you there. That is, to California. Now you want me to turn over my train to somebody else. Well, I'm going to show you I can be bigger about this than any of you. Have you men sounded out the rest of the folks? Do they want me to step down, too?"

"We haven't sounded out anybody," Fuller replied.

Cather laughed lightly.

"Mister Hammond must be losing his touch," he said. "Used to be he'd cook up something, like that last scheme of his that went sour, then he'd kinda sneak around where I couldn't see what he was doing, stir people up and then spring his idea on me. McBride must be responsible for the change in him. McBride must have thrown a scare into him. He's walking softly now."

"Aw, now, Will," Fuller began protestingly.

"You people made a deal with me," Cather continued disregarding Fuller and his attempt to say something. "If you think I haven't done my part, you've got the right to want out of our deal. If the others in the train feel the same way you do, let them say so, and I'll step down and let somebody else take over."

"You really mean that, Will?" Fuller asked. "That if the majority of the folks want to make a change, it will be all right with you?"

" 'Course I mean it."

Fuller turned to the men flanking him.

"Come on, you fellows," he said. "Long as Will is willing to be fair about this, we'll be fair with him. We'll keep out've things. We'll tell the others what's up, but we'll leave the decision to them. If the majority still want Will to run things, that'll be that. But if they go along with our idea and they agree we ought to have somebody

79

else take Will's place, they'll get somebody else. Come on."

Hammond had stood by quietly. He seemed to be stunned rather than simply surprised by Cather's willingness to accept the train's decision. Obviously he had expected Cather to put up a fight to maintain his hold on the train. That he hadn't, had left Hammond speechless. The others, led by Fuller, strode off. Slowly Hammond turned, looked back at Cather rather oddly, perhaps unbelievingly, then he trudged away.

"Well?" Cather demanded. "Go on. Say it."

Raines shrugged.

"What for?" he countered. "You know doggoned well you won't do what I tell you. So what's the use?"

"How do you know what I'll say till you've tried me?"

"All right, Will. I'll tell you what I think and you can take it or leave it. Unless you do something, and in one helluva hurry too, you're gonna find yourself out in the cold."

"Go on," Cather commanded.

"I think you'd better hustle down that line of wagons and start buttonholing people and speaking your piece. Everybody knows you know more about running a train than Hammond will ever know. But people forget things. So you'd better start reminding them. If you don't Hammond will sell them a bill of goods and he'll wind up with the train and you'll find yourself on the outside looking in. Or maybe you think you'll like takin' orders from Hammond when he takes over?"

Cather shook his head.

"I'm not takin' orders from anybody," he said evenly. "As for me buttonholing people and reminding them of anything, that's out. I'm staying put right here. If those folks," and he waved his hand in the general direction of the lined-up wagons, "are stupid enough to fall for anything Hammond tells them, he can have the train and all the headaches that go with it. Now what d'you think of that, Mister Raines?"

"I think you're a stubborn old coot," Raines retorted, "and maybe you ought to get what's coming to you."

"Thanks," Cather said dryly.

"I'm not finished yet."

Cather grinned at him. "That's what you think."

Raines pretended he hadn't heard him.

"I'm used to you now," he said, "so I suppose it'll be the natural thing for me to do."

Cather looked at him blankly.

"Trail along with you," Raines explained. " 'Course I know I'll be sorry for it sooner or later, but what the heck?"

Cather bristled and Raines hastily looked away. He did not want Cather to see the grin on his face.

"I don't need anybody to trail along with me," Cather answered indignantly. "You or anybody else. I'm not that old that I need someone to wet-nurse me. So you go chase yourself, you . . . you wall-eyed young pup."

"Nope," Raines said with exasperating calm. "And don't try to flatter me. It won't do any good. I'm stuck with you and that's that."

Cather was silent for a long moment, thoughtfully silent too, and Raines peered at him wonderingly. Suddenly, though, Cather grinned again.

"All right," Raines said. "If it's that funny, let me in on it too."

"Something just came to me and it struck me funny."

"I'm listening."

"Bill, what do you figure will happen when Hammond takes over the train?"

"O-h, he'll probably do something hare-brained like he did before."

"'Course he will, you idiot!" Cather exploded. "D'you think I need you to tell me that? Hey, I hired you, didn't I?"

Raines nodded and asked: "But what's that got to do with . . . ?"

"Those people," and again Cather waved his hand trainwards "They didn't hire you. I did. To work for me. And I've been paying you out've my pocket. Now if you haven't already figured out what I'm leading up to, you aren't as smart as I think you are. When I get the sack, you get sacked too. I won't need you any longer. Now tell me, Mister Raines, just what do you aim to do about that?"

"Nothing. I don't aim to do a blamed thing about it."

"Then don't you go telling me to do something, you young so-an'-so!" Cather yelled.

* * *

Anna and Katey Heydrich were sitting on the driver's seat of their wagon, while Kurt, his back turned to them, leaned against the front wheel, his eyes fixed interestedly on a group of people some twenty feet away. All of them seemed to be talking at the same time and Kurt could hear angry voices raised.

"What will we do, Mama?" Katey asked.

Kurt turned his head and lifted his eyes to his daughter. "Do?" he repeated. "For now we do nothing. We

82

will wait and see. Then when we see, it will be time enough for us to do."

Katey leaned forward.

"But, Papa," she said. "If everyone decides to go along with that Hammond man, we can't do anything else but go with him too."

"Everyone will not go with Hammond," Kurt said evenly. "There are many who do not like him, and even more who do not trust him."

"You're one of them, aren't you? You don't like him either, do you?"

"He talks too much," Kurt replied, "and too loud."

"Papa is right, Katrina," Anna said. She patted her daughter's hand. "We will wait and see. Then we can decide."

"Hammond comes," Kurt warned. "Quiet."

He squared around again against the wheel. Hammond came striding up to him. He nodded to Kurt, raised his eyes to Anna and Katey and touched his hat to them.

"I suppose you folks know what's going on without me having to tell you," he began.

"Yes, we know," Kurt answered.

"Good. Saves me the job of having to tell my story all over again, and the Lord only knows I'm about talked out. You folks are throwing in with the rest of us, right?"

"No," Kurt said bluntly. "That is not right."

Hammond's expression reflected his surprise. Kurt's eyes did not waver when they met Hammond's.

"Well," Hammond said with a curious heaviness in his voice. "If that's the way you people feel about it, all right. I kinda thought that after all the delays we've had to put up with, all the burnings and killings we've had to stand for, that anything would be an improvement. Guess I was wrong."

There was no comment from the Heydrichs'. Hammond looked from one to the other; when no one said anything, he shrugged, turned on his heel and stalked away.

Then minutes later a horseman rode up to the wagon, drew rein and slacking a little in the saddle, said to Kurt:

"Understand you and your family are gonna trail along with Cather. That right?"

"Yes," Kurt acknowledged. "That is right."

"I'm stringing along with him too," the man said. "You got anything in Cather's strong-box? If you have, hustle over and get it. Cather wants the folks who are stringin' along with him to come get their stuff, because he's turning the box over to Hammond. Better get over there now, Heydrich."

Kurt hurried away. The mounted man wheeled his horse.

"Please," Anna called, and the horseman pulled up again and looked at Anna. "There are many who have refused to go with Hammond?"

"Oh, about twenty, maybe twenty-five," the man answered. "The Andersons, the Turners, the Kellys, the . . . the Stevenses. I kinda forget for the minute who the others are. But all told we'll probably have about twenty-odd families left. The Howells are staying with Cather. Just remembered that. I was kinda surprised to hear it, because Tom and Hammond were pretty thick there for a while. But you never know, huh?"

"There is a young lady," Anna said. "Her name is Taylor, I think."

"Taylor?" the man repeated thoughtfully. He rubbed his chin with the back of his hand. "Lemme see now.

Taylor. O-h, sure . . . Peggy Taylor. She the one you mean?"

Anna smiled.

"Yes. She is the one."

"Peggy's staying with us, too." He grinned at Anna. "It figures she would being that Bill Raines is stringing along with Cather. I hear tell those two are planning to get married soon's we get a breathing spell. Just goes to show you that burning and killing don't mean a thing when two people have something on their minds."

He laughed and rode off, leaving Anna staring after him. But a minute later he came loping back.

"Look," he said to Anna. "When Hammond and those throwin' in with him pull out, you folks stay put. After they've gone we'll all pull up."

He rode off again. Anna and Katey looked at each other. Suddenly Anna's right hand flashed upwards, then it came sweeping down again in a resounding slap on Katey's cheek. The girl's head jerked back; for a moment she was stunned, speechless, incapable of any movement or show of emotion.

"You fool!" Anna said thickly. Katey's hand crept up to her tingling cheek. She touched it gingerly. "For you I am nice to this Raines. But what good does it do? No good. And why? Because you sit and wait and you dream, and while you do nothing, this girl, this nobody, she gets him. Sometimes you make me so mad, I could . . . "

With a sob, Katey leaped to her feet. Instinctively Anna thrust out a restraining hand, but there was no stopping Katey. She brushed off her mother's hand. Then with incredible swiftness she gathered her skirts together, lifted them, stepped on the wheel and jumped down, wheeled around the wagon and fled.

"Katrina!"

There was no response. Halfway up out of the wide seat, Anna was motionless for perhaps an instant, then she sank down again. She sat quietly, hunched over with her shoulders rounded and sloping. She did not look up when Kurt returned and climbed up and settled back next to her. Suddenly he realised that Katey was not there.

"Katrina," he said. "She has gone to bed already?"

"No."

Kurt gave his wife a long, questioning look.

"You do not feel so good, Anna?" he asked.

"Oh, I'm all right. It's Katrina."

"She is sick?"

"I don't know what she is," Anna answered. She sat up. "All of a sudden she stood up, jumped down from the wagon and ran."

"Our Katrina did that?" Kurt asked. He was surprised and his voice reflected it. "I do not understand. And you have no idea why she did it?"

"I don't know, unless it was because I slapped her."

"O-h," Kurt said. "I see now. And why did you slap her?"

"Because she made me mad."

Kurt drew a deep breath.

"You know, Anna," he said quietly, "there are times when you make me mad. You know that? But I do not slap you."

Anna was silent.

"I think you should go and look for her," Kurt went on, quietly as before. "Now, Anna."

"Kurt, I am tired. She will come back. It is night, so she cannot go far."

He climbed to his feet and stood over her.

"Since you are tired, go to bed," he said. "I am not tired, so I will go look for her." He climbed over the wheel and let himself down to the ground and stood looking up at his wife. "You will not slap her again, Anna. You hear? I will not have it."

He walked off without waiting for her reply.

Hammond's followers were on the move. Their wagons lumbered by and Kurt hurried between two of them. Then turning he peered up at each wagon as it came abreast of him, eyeing those on the driver's seat hopefully. It was twenty minutes later, after the last wagon had passed him, that he turned away and came face-to-face with Raines.

"Excuse me," he said. "Perhaps you have seen my daughter?"

Raines shook his head.

"No," he answered. "But isn't she with your wife? Usually they're together."

"Katrina is not with her."

Raines looked hard at him. He sensed that there was something wrong and instinctively sought to reassure Heydrich.

"Oh," he said. "I wouldn't worry too much. It's night and nobody wanders off very far in the dark. Chances are by the time you get back to your wagon, she'll be there too."

Kurt did not move.

"Look," Raines said hopefully. "Maybe she's visiting in one of the other wagons. You have a look around.

87

Meanwhile I'll keep an eye out for her too. I'll stop by later on and check with you. All right?"

Kurt nodded and trudged away. Raines followed him briefly with his eyes.

"Wonder what happened?" he mused to himself. "Mama and daughter have always seemed to be thicker than thieves. Now all of a sudden . . . "

He cut short his musing and strode on down the line and found Cather directing the moving up of the remaining wagons.

"Looks like we've got more wagons left than we figured," Raines commented as he stopped at Cather's side.

"Yeah," Cather answered. "How come?"

"Looks to me like some of those we didn't figure on changed their minds and stayed on."

"H'm," Cather said, but that was all.

The wagons moved, closing up the gaps left by those that had pulled out after Hammond. Together Cather and Raines started trudging up the line again when there was a distant burst of gunfire. The two men stopped as one and looked at each other. Men with rifles in their hands appeared. They looked at Cather, who shook his head.

"That isn't any of our affair," he said quietly. "It might be a trick to get us to leave our wagons and rush to help Hammond and leave the way open to somebody to come swoopin' down here instead. And if it isn't a trick and it's the real thing, Hammond has enough men with him, fact is, more than we have, to stand off McBride or whoever else it might be that's trying to raid him. So we're staying put. Only we'll get ourselves set for trouble if it should come our way."

A murmur of agreement ran through the men who had gathered around Cather.

"Some of you men get the women and kids out've their wagons and under them," he continued. "You other men hustle out a ways, say about twenty or thirty feet, get down in the grass as low as you can and have your rifles ready. If our friend McBride or anybody else decides to come pay us a surprise visit, open up on him soon's you spot him coming. That way we can get in some good licks at him before he comes too close. And if things begin to get too hot out there for you to handle, make your way back here. By that time we'll be ready to take him on and give it to him good. Go ahead, you fellers."

The men scattered. Cather turned quickly to Raines.

"Bill, you take the tail end of the train," he instructed. "I'll take the front end. Between us we ought to be able to keep things under control."

"Right," Raines answered, wheeled away from him and darted away.

The distant thunder of gunfire slackened off, swelled and fell off again. Then the westward sky brightened and glowed, and anxious eyes probing it knew that that meant one thing—fire. There was no need to tell anyone watching that Hammond's train had run into trouble while it was rumbling on. Probably it had been ambushed, and the deepening crimson in the night sky was an indication of what had happened. The firing continued in its original pattern; it swelled and fell off and broke out anew in a furious roar, and died down again. It was fully an hour before it faded out altogether.

It was midnight when Cather strode down the line in

search of Raines. When they came together, Raines asked:

"Think Hammond beat them off?"

"That's what I was gonna ask," Cather said. "He probably did though. But what I'm wondering is how many lives and wagons it cost him."

There was a light step behind them and when they turned they found Anna Heydrich looking up at them.

"You'd better get back to your wagon, Ma'am," Cather told her. "It isn't safe out in the open, you know."

"Wait a minute, Will," Raines said quickly. "I think I know what Mrs. Heydrich wants. It's something about your daughter, isn't it? That she's turned up and that she's all right?"

"I do not know," Anna replied. "Since I have not been able to find her, I hope now she is with her father. Perhaps you have seen my husband, Kurt?"

"Y-es, I saw him," Raines said. "Only that was quite a while ago. Hours ago. Hasn't he been back to the wagon since then?"

Anna shook her head.

"Tell you what, Mrs. Heydrich. Suppose you go back to your wagon and wait there while I go have a look around? Then I'll come over and let you know what I come up with. All right?"

Anna seemed undecided.

"That makes sense to me," Cather said to her. "You leave things in Bill's hands, Ma'am. He'll take care of them."

Anna held her gaze on him for a moment. Then she turned slowly, wearily and plodded away.

"What's this all about.?" Cather asked, turning to Bill.

"I don't know exactly, Will. But earlier this evening her husband came up to me and wanted to know if I'd seen their daughter. You know her, Will. A good-looking girl with blonde hair almost like her mother's."

"I've seen her," Cather said, nodding. "But I've never said anything to her. Never had occasion to."

"I have an idea that mama and daughter had some words, and Katey, or Katrina as they call her, probably got peeved and went off somewhere to sulk. But where in blazes she went to, I'm damned if I know."

"But what about papa? Where d'you suppose he is?"

"You've got me there, Will. 'Less he's still out looking for Katrina."

"The range is a helluva big place to have to go look for somebody," Cather commented. "And at night . . ." He didn't finish. He simply shook his head.

"Think you can handle things for both of us while I go looking for Katrina?"

Cather sputtered indignantly and the youth laughed and walked off.

CHAPTER VII

KATEY HEYDRICH'S pent-up emotions overcame her as she stumbled away from her mother's wagon. She was sobbing hysterically and her thoughts were confused and incoherent. Like a thoroughly frightened child who had been punished without understanding why she had been punished, she plunged away blindly, seeking instinctively to put distance between the one who had lashed out at her and herself. She came around the wagon and skidded to a stop. There was movement and excitement all around her. The train was dividing itself in two, and those who had chosen to accept Hammond's leadership in preference to continuing under Will Cather were already on the move. The excitement made Katey forget her own trouble for a moment, and she watched with interest as big, top-heavy prairie schooners and equally big farm wagons that were more solidly built rumbled past. The tailboard of one wagon was down, and every time the wagon lurched the tailboard swung free and then came thumping down against the rear wheels. Katey's eyes ranged past the tailboard to a length of thick rope that hung just inside the wagon from the curving top of its framework and which dropped to within an inch or two of the flooring.

She gathered her skirts together and darted after the wagon, and when the rope swung out she flung up both hands and grabbed it and leaped upward off the ground and into the wagon. She collided with a heavy packing case that refused to give way before her and went sprawling in the wagon's dark interior. Fortunately she did not cry out—fortunately, because a man came running up to the wagon, swung the tailboard up, and it slammed into place.

"All right!" she heard the man yell. "It's up. You can go ahead now!"

A whip cracked and the horses pulling the wagon quickened their pace. Katey got up on her knees and huddled there. She peered around the packing case. Fortunately, too, the canvas curtain at the front of the wagon hung full length, shutting out the driver from the rest of the wagon, and Katey, regaining her composure, breathed easier. Slowly she sank down on the floor, rested her back and head against the case. When the wagon lurched, the case started to slide towards the tail and Katey had to brace herself against it to hold it in place.

She heard hoofbeats and raised her head. There was no curtain at the rear of the wagon, and she could see out very clearly by peering over the top of the raised tailboard. She became aware of another wagon following directly behind them, then of other wagons behind the second one. She wondered if the people in the second wagon could see her. She decided they could not, because she could not see them. A horseman came up abreast of the second wagon, and he and the driver talked briefly but indistinctly; that is, as far as Katey was concerned. Then the horseman clattered past.

"Hey, Hammond!" Katey heard him call again. "You going to keep going right straight through the night?"

"Yeah," came the answer in a voice that Katey recognised as Hammond's. She caught her breath when she realised that Hammond's voice had come from the front of the wagon in which she was riding. "We've got a helluva lot of time to make up, and I'm going to push these danged horses till we get to where we're headed for or they drop."

The horseman did not answer; he simply wheeled his mount and rode back along the line of wagons.

Katey had not given a thought to her parents. Now she thought of them, and when Anna's face flashed through her mind, her lips tightened. She would never forgive Mama, she told herself. As for her father, she was not angry with him. Papa had always been kind to her. In fact, now that she thought of it, she could not recall ever having seen Papa angry. Poor Papa, he would feel badly about losing her. Mama would not; she was hard and unbending. They would never see Katey again. When she got to California, she would disappear altogether. Perhaps after a while she would manage to get word to Papa that she was alive and well, but she would warn him that he was not to breathe a word of it to Mama. Mama had to be punished. There were no two ways about that. She would make herself strong and unbending too, and then maybe one day Mama and she would meet. Her eyes gleamed for an instant. She would live just for that day. She did not know what she would do when the day arrived; she would worry about that later on.

Then a thought came to her which made her sit up.

She had no money and the only clothes she had were the ones she was wearing. What would she do when she got to California? The thought frightened her. She had never been in such a predicament. Whenever she had needed anything, there had been Papa to turn to, or Mama. She would not think of Mama again, she told herself. She would think only of Papa. Well, there was no sense in worrying about it now. California was a long way off. The rumbling wagon made her drowsy and finally her eyes closed. She opened them again shortly, but only briefly, because the motion of the wagon soon lulled her to sleep.

She did not open her eyes when she felt herself being lifted and carried and then being put down again. She felt her head being raised and something soft being placed under it, then a blanket was draped over her. She sighed deeply, contendedly, and turned over on her side. Then a hand touched her, brushed her hair back a bit from her face. It was a big hand; it was her father's, she told herself, and she smiled in her sleep. She had known all along that Papa would find her, she was happy again. In her dreams she imagined herself back on the farm in Illinois. She was a little girl again. She was in bed in her own room. And she was sniffling. Mama had scolded her for something or other and had finally sent her off to bed without her supper. She had cried herself to sleep, only to wake up when she felt her father's hand stroking her hair. She bent towards him and he lifted her gently into his strong arms, kissed her and held her tight for a moment. Then when he tried to put her down again she reached up, got both of her chubby arms around his neck and clung to him. The scene faded out. A tear dampened her cheek.

She felt the hand on her again, only this time it turned her around. She did not object. She felt lips brush her cheek and she sighed. A strong arm imprisoned her, held her tight. A scream formed on her lips, and was stifled when a heavy hand was clapped over her mouth, bruising her lips.

"Listen a minute," a man's voice whispered in her ear. She tried to squirm away, but there was no escaping him. "Use your head. I'm running this train, and what I say here goes. If you act up, I'll boot you out of this wagon, and then where'll you be? Out on the range with nobody within fifty miles to hear you or help you. If you're nice to me, maybe when we get to California, I can do something for you. But that's up to you. Now what'll it be, huh?"

She pulled away suddenly, and brought her knee up hard. The man gasped, and in that instant she had whipped off her covers, scrambled to her feet, flashed to the canvas curtain and thrown it back. She never knew how she managed to get over the driver's seat, over the high wheel and down to the ground, but she did. And then she began to run.

"Come back here, damn you!" she heard an angry voice cry after her, but she ran even faster.

She heard pounding feet behind her as she fled along the line of plodding wagons.

"Hey!" a man's voice called. "What'n blazes is going on around here?"

She tripped over a half buried rock and fell heavily. She was panting for breath now, and she fought her way up to her knees when a pair of arms caught her again and locked around her, lifted her. She screamed and clawed her captor, and he cursed her and put her down and lashed out at her with his fist. The punch was a cruel one. It struck her squarely in the face, and she sobbed and fell. Then, as the man bent over her again, she screamed: "Papa!"

He dragged her to her feet. She fought him off again and he struck her a second time, a savage blow that felled her.

"Well?" he demanded. "Had enough?"

She stirred, groaned, and he grunted.

"Come on," he commanded. "Get up on your feet and stop whimpering."

He lifted her to her feet, steadying her a bit. She kicked him suddenly, broke away from him and fled. He ran after her. She heard approaching hoofbeats and she ran faster, fighting all the while for her breath. The hoofbeats swelled.

"Papa!" she screamed. "Papa!"

A horseman rode up out of the night and pulled his mount to a stop.

Katey's captor overtook her, caught her by the arm and spun her around, and slapped her across the face. Katey screamed again and tried to pull away from him. He slapped her a second time, a third time. Other men ran up.

"That you, Hammond?" one man asked pantingly.

"It's him all right," another man said. "But what the heck's the matter with him? He gone loco or something?"

Hammond, holding Katey by the arm, turned and glared at the men.

"Get back to your wagons," he said gruffly.

The men did not move.

"G'wan!" he hollered. Katey began to struggle again and he cuffed her soundly. "I'll break your neck!"

She butted him with her head, and he lost his grip on her and she whirled away from him. The horseman swung himself out of the saddle. Katey flew towards him, with Hammond in mad pursuit.

"Papa!" she cried desperately. "Papa!"

There was an awakening bellow from the horseman. He rushed forward, and caught Katey in his arms.

"Katrina, baby!"

"Oh, Papa!" Katey gasped, clinging to him. Then she began to sob again, broken and hysterically. "That man, he beat me!"

Hammond rushed up and skidded to a stop. Kurt Heydrich spun Katey behind him. She went careening over the grass and fell on her hands and knees. Kurt lunged for Hammond, grabbed him by the shirt-front, then, holding off at arm's length, smashed Hammond in the face with a sledge-hammer fist. Hammond struggled to break Heydrich's grip, but there was no escaping Kurt's fury. He battered Hammond savagely, ruthlessly, with every punch landing in Hammond's face with a sickening, crunching sound. Hammond finally collapsed and sagged against Kurt, but the big man dragged him up and smashed him furiously half a dozen times more; then he simply cast him aside. Hammond toppled over in a limp heap.

Katey was on her feet now. Kurt turned and strode up to her, took her in his arms again and held her tight.

There was a sudden yell.

"Look out!" a man shouted. "He's got a knife!"

Kurt pushed Katey away. He turned as Hammond, a knife gleaming in his upraised right hand, came hurtling over the grass. Kurt met him head on. Hammond's right arm was suddenly thrust high over his head. There was a panting struggle for a moment, a crunching sound again, and the knife fell out of Hammond's hand. The men who were watching saw Kurt seize Hammond in his arms, and crush him in a bear hug, heard Kurt grunt, then heard an agonising scream from Hammond as his spinal cord snapped. Kurt released him and Hammond sagged brokenly to the ground. Kurt went back to Katey, lifted her in his arms, carried her back to his horse and swung her up into the saddle as lightly as if she were a tiny child, then climbed up behind her. Slowly they rode away into the night.

They had covered probably a mile when there was a sudden outburst of rifle fire from Hammond's train. Kurt reined in, twisted around and looked back. Katey sat up, too; then she pointed skywards. There was a sudden glow in the night sky; then flames climbed high into the blue. Kurt grunted.

"We will go on," he said, and Katey sank down against him.

Slowly, as before, they rode steadily eastward. The roar of rifle fire swelled and faded, arose and died out, broke out anew only to slacken off again and finally, probably half an hour after, a deep, oppressive silence settled over the darkened range. Kurt did not look back again. Katey's head was bowed and nodding against his chest; gently he moved her, brought her closer to him. Her head slipped into the hollow of his left arm. After a while he bent over her.

"Katrina," he said softly.

There was no response. He was satisfied that Katey was asleep. His arm tightened around her.

* * *

Will Cather was standing near the Anderson wagon at the head of the train when Kurt Heydrich rode up.

"Hello," Cather said, and strode over. He looked at the sleeping girl in the saddle in front of Kurt; then he looked up and smiled. "Found her all right, eh? Good thing. Your wife's just about out've her mind with worry. She's been popping in and out of her wagon like a jack rabbit every time she thinks she hears hooves."

Kurt said nothing.

"You see anything of Bill Raines in your travels?" Cather asked.

"Yes," Kurt said. "We met him on the range. He went on to Hammond's train."

"Uh-huh." Will said, nodding. "That's what I figured he'd do once he knew your daughter was all right. Speaking of the devil, how bad did Hammond catch it?"

"Bad," Kurt said quietly. "Very bad."

He nudged his horse with his knees and the animal moved slowly down the line of wagons. Cather turned, following him with his eyes.

"Didn't like the way he said that," he muttered. "Wish

to blazes Bill'd get back so I'd know how 'bad, very bad' really is."

He heard a step behind him and turned around. Peggy Taylor came towards him from the Anderson wagon.

"What's the matter?" he asked. "Couldn't you sleep?"

"No," she answered. "I've been twisting and turning all night long, and I was afraid I'd wake Mrs. Anderson, so I got up and got dressed. When do you think Bill'll get back?"

"Oh, he ought to be along 'most any time now," Cather said. "How'd you know he'd gone?"

Peggy smiled.

"I'd know his horse without seeing him," she said. "He has a funny way of snorting, and lots of other funny mannerisms, and after a while it's easy to recognise him when he goes by."

"You should have put on something over your dress," Will said. "It's blowing up."

"Oh, I'm quite warm. Listen."

They turned as one towards the open range that spread away before them.

"I don't hear anything," Cather said.

Peggy was motionless.

"Oh, yes," she said presently. "Didn't you hear a snort? I will admit it sounded more like a sneeze than a snort, but it's Bill all right."

"I sure hope so."

Then a shadowy horseman came riding out of the darkness, whirled up to the train, and jerked his mount to a stiff-legged stop when he saw the two figures standing beyond the first wagon.

"Hi, you two," he called. He swung himself out of the

saddle, hitched up his pants, and came striding up to them.
He looked at Peggy and frowned. "How come you aren't
where you ought to be at this hour?"

Peggy smiled at him.

"I couldn't sleep."

"You couldn't, eh? I could sleep for a week!"

He chucked her under the chin.

"Look," Cather said. "I don't like to bust this up, but
if you don't mind, Bill, I'd sure like to know how Hammond made out."

"Didn't Heydrich tell you?"

Will Cather snorted.

"He didn't tell me a thing. When I asked him how bad
Hammond caught it, all he said was, 'Bad. Very bad.'
How bad is very bad, Bill, in terms of people and things,
say like wagons, huh?"

"In the case of Hammond's outfit, sixteen wagons and
twenty people, half of them women and children," Raines
said quietly. "McBride really gave it to them this time."

"And how," Cather said grimly. "Looks like he's going
to follow us clear into California. Blast that Hammond!
I ought to break his fool neck for talking those folks into
following him."

"You can forget about Hammond."

"Y'mean they've given him the boot?"

"Hammond's dead."

Cather's head jerked up.

"Oh," he said. "Dead, eh?"

"Yeah. Only it wasn't McBride who did it. It was
Kurt Heydrich."

Peggy caught her breath. Cather simply stared at him.

"Heydrich?" he repeated. "How come?"

"It isn't a pretty story," Raines said. "So you can do without the details for now."

"H'm," Cather mused. "Heydrich, eh? Now that I think of it, he's a big man all right. Big enough to take on a grizzly. Must've had a damned good reason if he went to work on Hammond."

"You get a look at Katey?" Raines asked.

"She was asleep when I saw her," Cather answered. "Heydrich had her up in front of him. Her head was down against his chest and his arm was around her. But why'd you ask? Was there something the matter with her?"

"Plenty."

"Well, why'n blazes didn't Heydrich say so?" Cather retorted. "I'm supposed to be in charge here, and when anything happens to anybody, I'm supposed to be told about it. I better go see that Dutchman and find out what he's hiding from me."

Raines shook his head.

"I wouldn't, Will," he said.

"Why not?" Cather demanded.

"Leave them alone for now. You'll have plenty of chance to talk with them tomorrow. Besides, there isn't anything you or anyone else can do for them."

"Well . . . "

"Look, I told Hammond's people to stay put, and that we'd push on tonight and when we come along they can join up with us again. We ought to get going."

"Yeah, I suppose we'd better."

"I'll ride down and get things started. You take care of things at this end."

"Bill," Peggy said.

"Yeah?"

"Perhaps I can do something for Katey. You don't think they'll resent me, do you?"

Raines shrugged.

"I don't know. But if you don't mind trying, it might be just the thing. Go ahead. I'll look in on you later on."

Peggy went marching down the line.

"I'm going," Raines said to Cather.

He wheeled his horse and rode away.

The first Heydrich wagon was thoroughly darkened when Peggy came abreast of it. She stopped, looked up at it and considered for a moment, then decided to try the second wagon. She went on, came up to it and looked up. A thin ray of lamp-light seeped through the canvas drop. There was a big shadowy figure on the driver's seat.

"Mr. Heydrich," she called softly.

There was a movement on the wide seat.

"Yes?"

"May I talk with you for a moment, please?"

Kurt moved down the seat, swung himself over the high wheel and climbed down.

"Is there anything I can do?" Peggy asked.

Kurt looked at her. He was big and yet there was helplessness in the slope of his broad shoulders.

"Is she asleep?" Peggy asked.

He shook his head.

"No. She lies there, but she does not sleep."

"And Mrs. Heydrich? Is she with Katey?"

Kurt shook his head again.

"Katey does not want her."

"Do you think she'd mind if I came in and sat with

104

her?" Peggy asked. "Perhaps then she'd feel better, even doze off."

"You are very kind," Kurt said.

Peggy smiled up at him. She stepped past him to the wagon, climbed up over the wheel, slid over the driver's seat, dropped down into the wagon, lifted an end of the curtain, flipped it back and stepped inside. The curtain swung back into place behind her. A lantern that hung from an overhead stave furnished a yellowish and eerie light. Against a side wall of the wagon lay a blanketed figure, it's face to the wall. Peggy tiptoed forward, peered down for a moment, then dropped to her knees beside the girl.

"Katey," she said softly.

Katey turned slowly. Peggy gasped inwardly when she saw the girl's face. It was battered and swollen. One eye, the left one, was almost closed, and her lips were bruised and puffed. Peggy steeled herself. She smiled down at Katey.

"Is there anything you'd like?" she asked.

"No."

"A drink of water perhaps?"

"No, nothing, thank you."

Peggy bent over her, tucked in a strand of hair.

"Your hair is beautiful," she said. "It's like spun gold. If you won't let me get you anything, won't you please try to sleep?"

"I don't want to sleep."

"But you ought to try."

Katey did not answer.

"I'll be right back," Peggy said. She arose and went out. "Mr. Heydrich."

The tall figure standing near the wheel turned.

"I'll need some water, please," Peggy said. "And a good-sized piece of white cloth. A towel or an old shirt will do nicely."

"I will get them," Kurt said.

"Oh, yes. Have you any vinegar?"

"In the wagon. In a big bottle in the corner."

"Fine. Now will you get me the water and the cloth, please?"

"Right away. Katey, is she all right?"

"Of course," Peggy answered reassuringly. "In a couple of days' time, she'll be herself again. I can promise you that, Mr. Heydrich. Right now the best thing for her is sleep, and I think that once I get some cold vinegar compresses on her they'll soothe her and help her doze off."

"You are a fine girl."

"Thank you. And when Katey's herself again, I think we're going to be awfully good friends."

"That I will like very much."

The train was on the move when Bill Raines rode up alongside the first of the Heydrich wagons and looked up at the figure on the driver's seat.

"Hey, that you up there, Peggy?"

"Yes. And this is the laziest team of horses I've ever driven."

"Give them time. They're just waking up. They'll pick up as they go along."

"They'd better show some signs of life in a hurry," Peggy retorted, "or I'll wake them up with this whip."

"Hey, how come you're driving this wagon?"

"Someone had to. They tell me a team won't go unless it's driven."

106

"No fooling? Seems like someone's always coming up with something new. No telling what it'll be next. Say, where's the madam?"

"She's busy."

"Doing what? Sleeping, while you're driving?"

"Mama Heydrich is taking care of her daughter."

"Oh, yeah? Then things have changed since I was talking to Papa Heydrich a little while back. He told me you were nurse-maiding Katey and that Katey didn't want any part of her mother. How come the change? I don't suppose you had anything to do with that, did you?"

"A little, I suppose. After I made Katey comfortable, it wasn't hard to talk her into forgiving her mother and letting her take over for me."

"You're all right, Peg."

"Thank you, Mr. Raines. Thank you very much."

"Oh, think nothing of it," Bill said lightly. He rode alongside the wagon for another minute, suddenly swung his horse closer to it, swung out of the saddle, stepped lightly on the shaft and then pulled himself up on the seat beside Peggy. He grinned at her. "Haven't had much time for you lately. Seems like there's always something for me to do. And then when things quiet down and I get a breather, it's night and you've turned in."

There was no comment from Peggy.

"Been missing me a little?"

"A little," Peggy said airily.

"I think of you all the time."

Peggy said nothing.

"At night when it's so quiet and dark and I'm riding along, somehow I always find myself turning and looking at the Anderson wagon, knowing you're asleep in it, and wondering if you're dreaming and if it's ever about me."

The horses plodded along and the lines slackened a bit in Peggy's hands as she relaxed. Bill's arm came around her, tightened, brought her a little closer to him. He cupped her chin in his free hand, bent his head and kissed her gently on the mouth.

"Maybe I've never told you this before or said it right out," he said, "but I love you, Peg. I hope that kiss'll help you remember it."

He released her and got to his feet, turned and jumped down. His horse trotted up and Bill vaulted up into the saddle, spurred his mount and rode swiftly away.

CHAPTER VIII

IT WAS the middle of the morning when they sighted the waiting wagon train. There seemed to be little activity in the train, with scarcely a dozen persons moving about, and those appeared to be wandering aimlessly rather than purposefully. There were burned-out hulks of wagons at different points in the line, and Cather, riding at the head of his party with Raines at his side, shook his head and said:

"Look at that. I don't know what it does to you. But it makes me sick inside when I see what's happened to decent people who came out here with their hopes riding high only to have a skunk like that McBride slaughter them."

"Yeah," Raines said heavily. "I wish I had beaten him to death that day instead of letting him go."

"I've wished that a million times since that day," Cather said bitterly. "And I'll probably go right on wishing it as long as I know he's still alive."

They nudged their horses and sent them bounding

ahead, checked them again and slowed them to a walk when they rode in among the halted wagons. Grim, lined, hollow-eyed faces looked at them from the wagons. A single horseman with a rifle cradled in his arms rode forward to meet them, nodded to them as they came together and reined in.

"All set to move on with us?" Cather asked him.

"All set," the man answered. "We buried our dead at dawn and we've been waiting around for you ever since."

They wheeled their horses, backed them out of the way between two wagons as the first of Cather's wagons rumbled up. It was the Anderson wagon and Mary Anderson was alone on the driver's seat. John Anderson came riding up at that moment, clattered past the wagon and rode the length of the Hammond train, wheeled around and beckoned to his wife to come on. Cather's wagons followed one behind the other. When the last one had passed, Raines, the mounted rifleman and he rode out.

"All right, folks," Cather called. "Fall in one at a time and follow us. When we're rolling, make it a double line same as usual. Let's go!"

Dust began to rise and mushroom overhead as the horses and wagons got under way. The big wheels bit into the ground and spewed dirt. There were the usual squeaks as warped wagon bodies and shafts and sweat-stiffened harness were jolted into movement. Presently the two trains were joined. Cather, waiting at the head of the line, halted the train.

"You folks in the wagon with the busted top," he yelled through his cupped hands "Pull out of line and come up here. The rest of you come on up too, so's we can form a double line!"

It was a matter of some ten minutes before the double line was formed and the train was ready to move on again. Then with Cather and Raines riding ahead of it and John Anderson behind them and a couple of strides ahead of his own wagon, and the mounted man bringing up the rear, the train moved westward. The country ahead and on both sides was a smooth carpet of rich green, a level tableland that stretched away as far as the eye could see.

"Bill," Cather said, shading his eyes with his hand. "Think we're still in Wyoming?"

"Nope," Raines said. "I think we've been out of it for days. 'Less I'm mistaken, this is Utah. The northern part of it. If I'm right, a couple of more days and we'll be hitting the Nevada line, and then we turn south."

"How far south?"

"Couple of hundred miles."

Cather lapsed into silence again. After a while Raines turned to him.

"Going to use guards and fires tonight?" he asked.

"They worked all right the last time, didn't they? Sure we'll use them tonight and every night for that matter."

"Will . . . "

"Yeah?"

"Think it'll be all right for me to take about ten men tonight and go riding?"

"Just riding, or looking for something, or is it somebody?"

Raines met his eyes and grinned.

"I've got an idea you're up to something I've been mulling over for a spell. Figuring on scouting around under cover of darkness in hopes of spotting McBride's camp and carrying the fighting to him?"

"That's about the size of it."

Cather grunted.

"I don't want any family men with me," Raines told him. "We might run into more than we can handle. And if we have to fight our way out've it, I don't want to be worrying about leaving some more families without their menfolk."

"Thanks to McBride," Cather said, "we've got a lot more than just ten men without families. So you shouldn't have any trouble picking out the ones you want. I only wish I could leave somebody in charge here and go along with you. That would be one ride I'd enjoy, even if I didn't come back from it. I'd make damned sure, if I had to cash in, that some of McBride's killers came with me to keep me company."

"We mightn't find them, you know."

Cather smiled grimly.

"Oh, you'll find them, all right," he retorted. "And when you do, Bill, give them something they won't forget."

"Leave that to us, Will. We've got a lot of good people to square up for with McBride."

They moved apart after that, and both rode grimly and thoughtfully silent. The hours passed slowly. But finally it was noon.

"Think we'd better give them a chance to eat," Cather said.

Together they rode back and halted the train. Cather stood up in the stirrups.

"All right, everybody," he called. "Half an hour to eat. Hustle it now."

They walked their horses back to the Anderson wagon.

Mary Anderson had just climbed down from the driver's seat.

"Well?" she demanded of Cather.

He looked at her.

"Huh?"

"You said half an hour, didn't you?"

"That's right."

"And you said for us to hustle it, didn't you?"

"Yeah. But what . . . ?"

"If you expect to have some coffee to wash down whatever I can manage to get together to eat, you'd better get down off that horse and hustle around to the back of the wagon and fetch me the coffee pot."

Cather grinned at Raines.

"Y'see what happens, Bill? All you've got to do is be nice to a woman, and that's all, brother. From then on she owns you." He eyed Mrs. Anderson for a moment. "How d'you know I want coffee, doggone it?"

"I don't," she answered quite calmly. "But I know I do, and I'm sure John does. And I suppose when you see us drinking ours, you'll want some too. So get the pot."

"See what I mean, Bill?" Cather asked, turning to him again.

Raines wheeled his horse.

"Hey," Cather demanded, turning after him. "Where d'you think you're going?"

"Be back directly."

Cather frowned.

"Have to go see that Peggy's all right this minute? Here I am showing you what happened to me just because I was nice and polite to a woman. But that isn't enough for you, is it? You're one of those who has to learn the hard way. You can't profit from somebody else's experience."

Raines grinned and rode down the line.

"Sucker!" Cather called after him. "Sucker!"

"Will Cather!" Mary Anderson said sternly.

Their eyes met for a moment; it was Cather's whose finally wavered. He muttered something that sounded a lot like 'Women, doggone th'm!' Then he hoisted himself out of the saddle and climbed down, hitched up his pants, shook his head and trudged around the wagon to the rear of it. Mary Anderson simply smiled.

Peggy Taylor was alone on the driver's seat of Anna Heydrich's wagon, her arms folded on her drawn-up knees and her chin resting on her arms. Raines rode up, looked at her for a moment, then he dismounted.

"You're supposed to be having a quick bite to eat," he said. "Or don't you go in for eating?"

She did not answer, gave no sign either that she had heard him. He climbed up and seated himself next to her.

"I'm not particularly hungry," she said and sat up.

He thrust out his long legs in front of him and rested his feet on the rump of one of the horses. The animal turned his head and looked at him.

"Well?" he demanded of the horse. The animal turned his head away. "What were you thinking about so hard, Peggy?"

"O-h, lots of things."

"For instance?"

"Bill, do you honestly believe we'll ever see California?"

"Course we will! Whatever gave you the idea we

114

wouldn't?"

"McBride," she said simply.

"McBride or no McBride, we'll still get there," he said

"All of us, Bill?"

"Maybe not all of us," he conceded. "But you can bet on it, Peg, there'll still be plenty of us left when we ride over the California line. McBride isn't going to stop us or beat us. He might make even more trouble for us than he has already. But he won't kill all of us off."

"It frightens me," Peggy said. "Every morning there are fewer people left alive and fewer wagons untouched by fire. How long can we go on like that, losing people and wagons so steadily? We're still a long way from California, weeks away, perhaps even months. Then I get to thinking that perhaps none of us will ever get through."

"Don't think things like that," he said sternly. He moved a little closer to her. "Look, Peg. We're going to make it. I know we are."

Her slender shoulder lifted in a wordless shrug.

"Did I ever tell you about our place in California?" he asked. "It's mine now, y'know Or have I told you that?"

"Y-es, I think you did."

"You've got something to look forward to. Seeing it, I mean. It's in a valley. Just about the most beautiful place you ever saw. And flowers? Every kind you ever heard tell of, they're there by the millions. And the California sun isn't like any other sun. Oh, it's bright and warm the way the sun is supposed to be. But what makes it different is that it doesn't burn right through like this one does. It makes everything look alive and happy, even makes you feel glad you're alive. Even the ground in California is different. It's so doggoned rich, anything can grow in it once it takes root."

She had squared back in the wide seat, her head lifted, listening, drinking in every word he was saying.

"Our house out there is something," he continued. "It's big and roomy and comfortable. 'Course it's been closed up for a couple of years now. But a little airing out and it'll be right the way it should be. Y'know anything about trees? California's famous for trees. Got all kinds, the biggest and the littlest. I like the evenings out there best of all. There's always a nice, cooling little breeze, so soft and gentle-like. When you're sitting outside under the stars, you can hear the breeze whispering to the grass and the flowers. The breeze lifts the fragrance from the flowers, and from the grass too, and carries it right up to you and sort of drapes it over you and you get the rich, sweet smell in your lungs, way down inside of you, in your hair, too, and in your clothes. I've never felt that way about anything anywhere else."

He slumped back and lifted his eyes skywards. Then he sat up again, reached over and took her hands in his.

"Now, look, Peg. Till we get there and you see everything for yourself, and just the way I've described it, you've got to keep your chin up and above all, you've got to keep telling yourself over and over again that we're going to get there."

"But, Bill, suppose . . .?"

"Yeah?"

She shook her head.

"Nothing, Bill. Forget it, please."

He looked disappointed.

"Still worried, huh, in spite of everything I've been

telling you? Not only about making it to California, but probably what you'll do there, huh? We-ll, I think I can do something about part of that worry. Relieving you of it, I mean. I've got it all settled in my mind that you're going to marry me, Peg. Have I got that right?"

She half-turned to him and smiled.

"You know I love you, Peg," he said. "You know that, don't you?"

"Yes, Bill. And I love you, too. And if it weren't for you, giving me the courage whenever mine falters and I get filled with doubts and misgivings, I don't know what I would do. I'll marry you, Bill, gladly and happily and whenever you want me to."

"Thanks, Peg," he said. He released her hands and got to his feet. "You stay put here. I'll be back in a minute."

She looked up at him wonderingly, but she did not ask the question that framed itself on her lips. He bent over and kissed the tip of her nose. He swung himself over the wheel and landed lightly on the ground and ran up the line of wagons. His horse, idling close by, started after him, overtook him, pulled alongside of him and ran along with him, the empty stirrups swinging a little wildly and thumping against his sides. The Andersons with Cather in the middle were sitting cross-legged in the grass near their wagon. They had finished eating and now they were relaxing. They looked up quickly, Cather rather concernedly, when Bill panted up to them. Apparently the excitement within Raines had communicated itself to his horse; the animal snorted and pawed the ground with an impatient hoof.

"What's the matter, Bill?" Cather demanded.

"Just want to ask you something."

Cather, halfway up, sank down again.

"Long as that's all," he said.

"Will, you're head man around here. You read a funeral service when one of our people is to be buried. Now suppose somebody wanted to get married? Could you marry them?"

Cather scratched the end of his nose with his thumbnail.

"I don't know, Bill," he answered after a moment's thoughtful silence. He turned to the Andersons, looked first at John, who shrugged, and then at Mary. "What d'you think, Mary? Think it will be all right?"

"I don't know why it wouldn't be," she said without any hesitation.

"There y'are, Bill," Cather said to him. "Mary usually knows what's what. So I guess it would be legal for me to marry somebody "

"Swell," Raines said.

"Wait a minute," Cather commanded. "Who are you asking for? Who's this somebody who's in such a sweat to get married that they can't wait till we hit California?"

Mary Anderson smiled.

"Never mind that, Will," she said. "Just tuck in your shirt while I go and get my bible. And Bill . . . "

"Ma'am?"

"Tell Peggy I'll be with her directly. John, will you put the dishes and things away, please?"

Peggy was sitting at the very end of the wide seat, looking anxiously up the line, when she spied Raines racing back to her. Quickly she moved to make room for him beside her. When he came panting up, but made no attempt to climb up, she looked at him wonderingly again.

"Wait till I get my breath," he wheezed. Then: "I don't want to take any chances. I want to make sure you won't be left on your own if you should get to California and I shouldn't. I want to know you'll be set, that you'll have a home and money. Peg, I just asked Will Cather to marry us. That all right with you?"

"Of course, Bill."

"I mean now."

She smiled gently.

"I'm ready, Bill."

He reached up for her. She came to him without delay. He lifted her easily over the wheel, turned with her and set her down on the ground. She touched her hair, smoothed down her dress while he watched.

"Do I look all right?"

"You look wonderful to me. O-h, Mrs. Anderson said to tell you she'll be right along."

"Where will you be?'

"Waiting for you with Cather and Mr. Anderson." He looked closely at her. "You won't be nervous and cry, will you?"

She smiled at him.

"No, Bill, I won't."

"Good girl," he said. "O-h, here she comes." He stepped back. "Be seeing you."

Cather, Anderson and Raines were standing together, hatless and a little awkward looking, when Peggy and Mrs. Anderson, the latter with her arm through Peggy's, came up to them. Cather, the bible in his hand and his big thumb holding it open at the page he was to read from, cleared his throat.

"Bill," Mrs. Anderson said. "Stand next to Peggy. John,

you stand behind Bill. All right, Will. You're supposed to face Bill and Peggy, you know. That's it."

Cather, having moved as Mary Anderson directed and now stood facing the two young people, opened the bible.

"Beats me," he muttered, "how some fellers can go out've their way looking for trouble."

"Will!" Mrs. Anderson said, and her husband grinned.

"Don't take him seriously, Mary," he told her. "He doesn't mean half of what he says."

Cather cleared his throat again.

"All right now," he announced. He read a couple of lines of the marriage service to himself, his lips forming the words. He frowned and suddenly jerked his head up. Peggy and Raines. "You mind if I make up what 1 have "Doggone it, Mary, the print's so blamed small, I can barely make it out. Look," he said, addressing himself to to say, long as you wind up married?"

Mary Anderson answered for them.

"Very well," she said, a little begrudgingly though. "But mind you, Will Cather. This is a marriage service you're officiating at. Not a christening or a funeral."

Cather closed the bible and put it in his left hand.

"God," he said, lifting his eyes skyward. "We ask you to witness this wedding and give it your blessing. The young people are Bill Raines and Peggy Taylor." He ranged a look around the small uneven circle of curious onlookers that had formed beyond the wedding party. "Anybody know of any reason why these two people shouldn't be married to each other?"

There was no response and Cather grunted.

"Take her hand, Bill," he instructed. "Then: "You, Bill Raines, d'you take this woman for your lawful wife, for better or for worse, in health and in sickness, for richer or poorer, till death do you part?"

"I do," Raines answered.

"And you, Peggy Taylor, d'you take this man for your lawful husband, for better or for worse, in health and in sickness, for richer or poorer, to love, honour and obey till death do you part?"

"I do."

"Where's the ring?" Cather asked, and levelled a look at Raines. "Haven't you got a ring, or didn't you know you were supposed to have one?"

"Of course he has a ring," Mrs. Anderson said. "John's holding it for him."

"Huh?" John Anderson said. "What do you mean I'm holding it for him? When did I get it and who'd I get it from?"

"Oh, dear," his wife said. "I thought I'd given it to you, John. But I've still got it. Here."

She held it out to her husband, a simple gold band. Anderson reached for it, took it from her and handed it to Raines. She turned to Peggy.

"It was my mother's," she said.

"Come on, Bill," Cather commanded. "Let's get this over with so we can get rolling again. 'Less you've changed your mind and want to back out before I pronounce the fatal words. What d'you say?"

"Will Cather . . . !"

Cather grinned.

"I was only fooling, Mary," he said. "Bill doesn't want to back out've this no more than Peggy does." He looked very solemn now. "Bill Raines and Peggy Taylor, I pronounce you man and wife. Bill, put the ring on her finger, kiss her, and that'll be that. You other folks hustle back to your wagons so's we can pull out of here. That means

121

you two love birds, too. O-h, here y'are, Mary. Here's your bible."

* * *

The night was dark and chilly. The train was shrouded in shadowy darkness and deep, sleepy silence save for the occasional milling about of a couple of tied-up horses that seemed unable to settle down for the night. They bumped one another, crowded against each other, then, curiously enough, they suddenly subsided and huddled together headbent. But a minute later both backed off almost as far as their tethering lines permitted, kicked and trampled one another, then ceasing their antics abruptly, came together again and finally stood still.

Shadowy figures with rifles slung over their shoulders paced about, stopping every now and then to probe the dark range beyond the train. Then they paced on again. A man came trudging down the line of wagons from the head of the train. It was Will Cather. A taller, leaner figure came towards him and Cather looked up at him in surprise and stopped.

"Hey, Bill," Cather said. "What in blazes are you doing up and around?"

"I've got something to do," Raines answered. "Remember?"

"Aw, forget it for tonight," Cather told him. "This is one night you oughtn'ta be thinking about anything but your . . . "

"I know," the tall youth interrupted. "But Peggy knows I've got a job to do and she isn't the kind to stand in the way of it. Besides she's asleep. So the sooner I get started, the sooner I'll be back."

Cather's shoulders lifted in a shrug.

"All right, Bill," he said. "If that's the way you want it."

"Keep an eye on her for me, will you, Will?"

" 'Course," Cather assured him. "She'll be all right. Just see to it that you are too."

"Got the papers I gave you to hold for me? The deeds to the ranch and the other things?"

"They're in safe hands. Mary Anderson's. You got your men all set?"

"They're probably waiting for me now," Raines said and turned away. "See you later, Will," he added over his shoulder.

"I'll be around," Cather responded.

He followed Raines with his eyes, saw him disappear behind a wagon and reappear almost at once leading a saddled horse. He watched Raines climb up astride the animal and wheel away. Far down the line other horsemen rode out from between wagons and trotted forward to meet Raines. When he motioned, they swung around and fell in behind him and rode out on to the shadowy range. For a minute or two Cather could hear the band's hoofbeats. But then they faded out, died away completely and everything was hushed and silent again.

CHAPTER IX

BILL RAINES twisted around and looked back at the troop of men strung out in single file behind him. Presently he dropped down again, settled himself in his saddle, suddenly jerked his horse to a stop, and whirled the startled animal around as the other horsemen came crowding up to him.

"Hold it a minute!" he called. "There's something cockeyed 'round here. We started out with eleven men all told, and all of a sudden there are twelve of us."

The men reined in. Raines swerved his horse away from the others, cut over and pulled up in the path of the last man, who was just riding up.

"Just a minute, Mister," he said. "Who are you and who invited you along on this party?"

The man laughed.

"Funny thing, y'know?" he said. "I was out exercising my horse, and all of a sudden you fellers came past me and I got the idea that I might just as well have company on my ride, so I fell in behind you and kind of tagged along. Hope I'm not butting in on anything."

Raines inched his horse up close to the other's mount. He peered hard at the man for a moment.

"Uh-huh," he said. "Thought there was something familiar about your voice. What's the idea, Howell?"

"Tell the truth, Raines, I overheard some of the boys talking about going calling on McBride tonight and—well,

I didn't want to be left out of it. But before you say any-thing, let me say something I've been meaning to say to you, only every time I go looking for you to say it, you aren't around. Thanks for fishing me out of the burning wagon."

"Forget it," Raines said. "You'd have done the same for me. You all right now?"

"Let me go along and you'll see."

"Looks like we're going to have to let you. Only there's one thing you've got to promise me."

"All right. What is it?"

"You've got a family to think about. Don't take any wild chances, no matter what we get into."

"It's a deal."

Raines wheeled his horse away and loped to the head of the party.

"Let's go," he called over his shoulder. "And stick close together."

The troop re-formed and fell in behind Raines as before. The range grass was thick and it muffled their horses' hoof-beats. They rode southwards steadily, a strung-out line of shadowy men and horses who seemed to lose their identity in the deep night light. A rider came spurring up and ranged himself alongside of Raines, who looked at him. It was Howell again.

"All right for me to ask what you're planning to do?" the man asked.

"Sure," Raines answered. "Kind of figured we'd swing in a circle and head north again. That way we can cover a lot of ground."

"Uh-huh. How d'you figure this McBride feller?"

"What d'you mean?"

"Think he holes up somewhere and kind of works out

of that one spot?"

"Heck, no. He's got to keep moving the same way the train does, so I figure he makes camp and lays low till it gets dark, and then he rides out and takes his whack at us. When he gets finished, he just turns around and hightails it back to camp, gets his sleep and moves on again in the morning. 'Course he's smart enough to keep far away from us during the day to make sure we don't spot him. But you can bet on it, Howell, he don't hole up. He's on the move all the time."

"Yeah, guess that's so."

"I'm just hoping that we can find his camp, sneak up on him and take a whack at him before he heads his outfit towards the train."

"Going to try to hit him and hurt him so he won't be able to do any hitting of his own."

"That's the general idea. Now all we've got to do is find him."

They rode along in silence for a time. Finally, Raines checked his horse. Howell looked at him quickly.

"See something?" he asked.

"Nope. Think we'll start swinging around now. We've come far enough for tonight."

They slowed their mounts to a trot. The other men rode up to them and looked at Raines questioningly.

"We're turning around," he announced. "We'll have to hope we run into something on the way back. Watch yourselves now."

They rode westward, not directly, but in a swinging arc. The night wind stiffened a bit and swept dirt into their horses' faces. Here and there a protesting horse shied out of line, but after a brief tussle the line was reformed and they went on. Presently they were riding directly north.

There was no conversation, no sound, nothing save an occasional creaking of saddle leather which was usually short-lived. Raines and Howell pulled their horses to a sudden stop and looked at each other.

"There they are," they said together. Raines turned quickly. "Hold it! Walk your horses up here!"

The other men came up to them.

"What is it?" one man asked.

"McBride," another answered simply.

"Oh," the first man said.

Far ahead of them they could see a camp fire burning brightly against the background of the dark night. Sparks spun upwards and darted across the sky, but their flight seemed unusually short. They dissolved into nothingness after a short climb.

"Good thing for us the grass out here's as thick as it is," Howell muttered, "or they'd have heard us coming and then we'd have had one heck of a swell shindig."

"What d'we do now?" someone asked.

"What d'you think?" another man retorted. "We came out here looking for them, and now that we've found them we're going to take a whack at them, of course!"

"Save the talk for later," Raines said. "Get down off your horses."

The men dismounted.

"Take your rifles," Raines ordered. "You'll need them."

Rifles were jerked out of saddle boots.

"Kneel down around me," Raines said. "That's it. Now look. We're going in for a fight, a quick one, just a couple of shots, then we're going to hightail away from here as fast as we can go. 'Course it won't do any harm if you make every shot count. The more of them we manage to knock off, the more of our own lives and the lives of the other folks we'll save. Every man will take his horse with him. Only you're going to lead your horses, not ride them. Half of you'll go one way, half the other way. Howell'll tag along with me. We'll hit them from the centre."

"Swell," Howell said.

"Circle around," Raines continued. "Pick a spot and leave your horse there, then creep forward on your hands and knees to say about thirty feet from the fire. Got that? Pick the man you're gonna shoot at, and when I give the word, let him have it, but good. When I holler, get the devil out again, hop on your horse and ride like blazes. We'll meet north of here unless something happens to us, and then it'll be every man for himself. Any questions?"

"I got one," a man said. "How about two quick shots for a signal to begin shootin' and two more for us to back-track and hightail it? If there's any excitement, sure as shootin' we won't be able to hear you holler."

"All right," Raines said. "Two shots to shoot and two more to quit. Get going and don't take too long getting there.

The men started away. Raines and Howell, squatting in the grass, watched them until they saw them start to swing in a circle as instructed.

"Come on," Raines said presently.

"Right with you."

They crawled forward slowly, delaying their advance in order to give the other men sufficient time to reach their positions. They took advantage of the brief delay to raise their heads for a quick look at the camp ahead of them.

"Look," Howell said. "Off to the left of the fire. Look at them horses! Must be forty or maybe fifty of them!"

"Uh-huh," Raines said. "So far I've counted more than twenty men layin' around the fire. Then there's a bunch of them near the horses."

"I see them," Howell grunted. "Looks like McBride's got himself a regular army."

They burrowed deeper into the grass and crawled ahead.

"Wait up," Howell whispered. "I got a small bunch of faggots. Somebody must've dropped them here."

"Uh-huh."

"Y'know," Howell said, "if we could light them and chuck them in among those horses, we'd sure raise plenty of hell with them."

"Wouldn't we though!"

"Got any ideas?"

"One idea," Raines whispered back. "How many faggots you got?"

"Oh, six or maybe eight. Why?"

"If you could light them all at one time and chuck them one after another, I could cover you and open up on them."

"Yeah, but let me throw them first." Howell twisted a bit, then grunted, an indication that he had found what he had sought. A tiny light sputtered in his hands and promptly went out.

"Try it again."

A second light flamed, sputtered and suddenly crackled.

"That did it!" Howell whispered excitedly.

"Give it a chance to start burning!" Raines told him.

Howell got up on his knees.

"Here we go!"

His right arm jerked backward. A flaming faggot streaked through the darkness and dropped squarely in the middle of a compactly bunched group of horses. There was a cry of fright and they reared up, backed and lashed out with their hooves at the burning branch that lay in the grass at their very feet. A second faggot came hurtling overhead, struck one of the horses a glancing blow, caromed off his back and fell sputtering beside him. The badly frightened animal whirled and fled, and the other horses followed suit. A couple of men sought to halt them by running out in front of them and waving their arms vigorously, but they were brushed aside. One man lunged for the bridle of a big white mare. He missed and went sprawling on his face. He tried to roll out of the path of an on-rushing horse when still another animal came pounding down upon him. The man disappeared beneath a flurry of flashing hooves.

Other men ran up and tried to calm the rest of the horses; they had almost succeeded in quieting them down when a third and fourth faggot fell among them. The panicky animals tramped the men, fought to get away, finally broke their tethering lines and, like a herd of stampeding steers, swept everything before them as they bolted off. Some of the horses ran a short distance, stopped and came trotting back; when the last of the faggots fell near them, they wheeled and darted off again.

There were scattered shots from some of McBride's men, who were just as badly shaken as the horses; they fired wildly, this way and that. Now Raines Colt roared twice and there was an immediate echo. Then rifles thundered a volley and raiders fell before the blast of gunfire.

The rifles thundered a second time and more men fell. One man pitched forward directly into the camp fire; another man grabbed him by the boot heels and dragged him out, straightened up, jerked out his gun, raised it, when a bullet hit him. He tottered, sagged and fell in a heap. Another man ran up and dropped a blanket over the fire; smoke belched upwards and he backed away choking. A rifle bullet struck him and he clutched at his chest; he turned slowly, and was plodding away when a second bullet hit him. He fell down, forced himself up, started off again when his legs gave way beneath him and he toppled forward a second time. But this time he did not get up.

Now the rifle-armed men sprawled in the grass and fired at the flashes of the attackers' rifles. The thunder of gunfire was deafening. Now, too, some of the horses returned. They came loping back, circled the camp, and some of them stopped squarely between the attackers and the attacked. Raines and Howell, sprawled out in the grass, halted their fire for a moment.

"I think we ought to get going," Raines said.

"Aw, take it easy," Howell pleaded. "We're doing all right, so why spoil the fun?"

"Well," Raines said; then he grabbed Howell's arm. "Back up!" he yelled.

A band of mounted men came out of nowhere, heading directly for them. Raines and Howell scrambled to their feet, wheeled and snapped a couple of discouraging shots. A man fell off his horse and a second rider slumped forward in his saddle; then he slipped out and toppled into the grass. A bullet ploughed the ground at Raines' feet. Another bullet whined by Howell's head, and he simply hurled himself the other way, fell awkwardly, scrambled to his feet again, cursing and shooting in a blind rage. Bullets fell all around them and Howell, forgetting himself completely, stood his ground and emptied his gun at the oncoming horsemen. Raines dragged him away. They reached their own mounts, got up on them somehow, dug their heels into their flanks and sent them bounding off. A single horseman came into view ahead of them. Raines fired twice and the man was lifted out of the saddle and hurled earthwards.

There was some shooting ahead of them and they could see shadowy figures astride horses, but there was too much gunsmoke and too much confusion, so they swerved away and rode eastwards for a time. Their horses seemed just as anxious as they were to put distance between McBride's men and themselves, and the animals flashed over the ground at a breakneck pace. Finally they found themselves far removed from the camp. The range was hushed and they slowed their horses to an easy lope.

"Hope the boys made it out of there all right," Raines said.

"They must've," Howell replied. Then he laughed. "Hey, we sure raised hell with them, didn't we?"

"Yeah. Seemed to me I could see McBride's men falling all over the place. Wonder how many we actually got?"

"Don't know. All I do know is that I got four or five for sure and three or four others who looked like they were hit real bad. You must've got even more than I did."

They rode westwards and then, after they had covered a couple of miles, turned northwards.

"What are you plannin' to do when we get to California?" Howell asked.

"I got a ranch."

"H'm, that's all right. Y'know, at first I had an idea I'd head northwards and try my hand at panning gold. Now I'm not so sure. I got a wife and a couple of kids, and that'd be tough living for them. I got to figure out some other way of makin' a living."

"Think you might like working on a ranch?"

"Oh, sure. And the kids'd love it. That youngest one of mine, Tommy, he's crazy 'bout horses."

"I can use a couple of good men. Will Cather's going to

be my foreman. The Andersons are coming with me, too. Think the Howells'd like to join us?"

Tom Howell jerked his horse to a sudden stop. Raines pulled up and looked at him quickly.

"You on the level?" Howell asked.

"The job's yours if you want it. Got a couple of small cottages behind the big house, and one of them can be yours. You think it over and let me know what you decide."

"I've thought it over."

Raines laughed.

"Already?"

"Yeah. The Howells are ready the minute you say the word."

"Swell. We'll consider it settled. You're on the payroll the minute we hit California."

"Hey, will it be all right for me to tell the Missus?"

" 'Course it will."

"She's been worrying about what's gonna happen to us when we get to California, and when I tell her we're gonna work for you and that Cather and the Andersons are gonna be part of your outfit, too, she'll be pretty doggoned happy. Thanks, Raines, for giving me a break."

"Forget it. Now suppose we get going again?"

They were within a mile or two of the train when they heard a whoop. There was a rush of hooves and then men came galloping up to them.

"Hey!" Howell yelled. "You all right?"

"And how!" a man answered. "How'd we do, Raines?"

"Fine," Raines replied. "I wouldn't want a better bunch to fight with."

"We sure raised ructions with McBride, didn't we?"

"Think you'll be up to making another surprise visit tomorrow night?" Raines asked.

"You can count me in on that party," Howell said.

"Me, too," another man chimed in. "I wouldn't want to miss it."

There was a general nodding of heads.

"Good," Raines said. "Now let's be on our way again. Cather'll be fit to be tied if we don't show up pretty soon. Come on."

Will Cather was beside himself when they rode up to the train. He came bustling up to Raines and shook a pudgy finger in the youth's face.

"Dammit!" he sputtered. "Where in blazes have you been, huh? I thought this was gonna be one of those one, two, three, bang affairs, and then you'd be back again. Dog-gone your ornery hide, start talking and talk fast!"

Howell nudged Raines.

"All right if I get out of here?" he asked. "I'm in a powerful rush to tell Amy."

"Sure," Raines said. "Go ahead."

Howell rode down the line of wagons.

"Hey," Cather said. "He's a married man, isn't he? And hasn't he got some kids? How come he was with you?"

"Look, you fellers," Raines said, turning to the other men. "You've done a swell job tonight. You've earned a good sleep. Why don't you go along and turn in?"

The men needed no urging. They wheeled their horses and rode away.

"Now," Raines said to Cather, "if you can shut up for exactly ten minutes, I'll tell you all about it."

*   *   *

Tom Howell unsaddled his horse, tied him up to the rear wheel, climbed up into his wagon, took off his boots, slung his hat aside, unbuckled his gunbelt and hung it up on a nail, took off his shirt and pants and dropped them on the floor. Then he inched his way to where his wife lay asleep with her blanket drawn up close around her and her face to the wall. He eased himself down beside her. She turned around instantly.

"Tom!"

"Sh-h-h! You want to wake the kids?"

"Are you all right?"

" 'Course I'm all right."

"Where were you?" she asked in a whisper. She moved closer to him. "Why didn't you tell me you were going off somewhere?"

" 'Cause I didn't want to worry you," he answered in a hushed tone. "Raines and a bunch of us went to pay that McBride a little visit. We should've done it right off; then we'd never have heard of him again. But we sure raised the devil with him tonight, believe me." He turned on his side, facing her. "Y'know, Amy, it don't pay to say you don't like somebody till you've really had a chance to find out what they're like. I learned that tonight. Take this feller Raines. You know how sore I was at him. Well, tonight I had a real good chance to see what he's made of, and he's all right. Fact is, he's a fine feller."

"I'm glad, Tom."

"Y'know, he's got a ranch to go to as soon as we hit California. He told me all about it. His father left it to him. Cather's goin' with him as foreman and the Andersons are going along, too."

Amy Howell offered no comment.

"Bet the kids'd love it if we had a chance to live on a ranch, wouldn't they?"

"Better than anything in the world."

"Wouldn't it be something if we got that chance, and

135

then saved our money and maybe after a while bought us
a little place that'd be all our own?"

She propped herself up on her elbows and peered at him
in the darkness.

"Tom Howell," she said finally, "you haven't been
drinking, I can tell that. But you're up to something.
What is it? I want to know this very instant."

He laughed softly, reached out, took her in his arms
and brought her closer.

"We're goin' with Raines, too," he said.

"Oh, Tom!"

"That's right," he continued. "Raines offered me a job
the same as he did Cather and Anderson, and told me to
think it over. I told him I didn't have to think it over for
one single minute. I accepted right then and there. He
laughed and said I was on the pay-roll the minute we
hit California."

She clung to him, her head on his chest.

"Oh, yeah," he said again. "Nearly forgot to tell you
the rest. Seems like there are some cottages on the place
and Raines said one of them would be for us. How d'you
like that?"

"Oh, I'm so happy, I could cry!"

His arms tightened around her as a tear rolled down her
cheek, and she turned her head away quickly. Her cheek
brushed his and he felt its dampness.

"Hey," he whispered. "Amy, honey, for Pete's sake!"

She bowed her head, rested it against his shoulder. She
sobbed for a moment softly, sniffled once or twice, then
the sobbing ceased. She turned to him again and slid down
beside him, pillowing her head in the hollow of his arm.

"All right now!" he whispered.

"Yes."

He smiled to himself. Women were curious creatures. They cried when they were happy, and cried when they were unhappy. She sighed once, and burrowed a bit deeper into the bed roll. He lay very still. He was thinking of California. He could almost see young Tommy astride a big horse.

"Amy," he said.

There was no response. She had dozed off. He closed his eyes, and presently he, too, fell asleep.

* * *

A few minutes after Raines had left him and climbed into the wagon to rejoin his wife, Will Cather came sauntering down the line of shadow-draped wagons. He glanced at each wagon as he passed. When he came abreast of the first of the Heydrich wagons, he stopped and looked up at it and grinned. He was re-living the wedding ceremony he had performed.

"Wonder if that Sally Higgins ever got married?" he mused. "I sure came close to gettin' hitched that time all right, 'bout as close as a man can come to it without windin' up married. She was nice, all right, but the minute her mother opened her mouth, I was looking for the nearest door. And her father, he listened to her for a minute, shook his head and went out. I went after him, only he walked out while I just about flew. I remember running into the old gent a couple of years later and having a drink with him and he shook hands with me and patted me on the back. That was the last time I ever had any thoughts about gettin' married."

A man climbed down from a nearby wagon and Cather eyed him curiously.

"S'matter?" he asked when he came up to him. "No

sleep in you tonight?"

The man looked at him and hitched up his belt.

"Oh, I could've done a job of sleepin'," he replied. "It was my wife who couldn't."

"Oh," Cather said.

"For two solid hours she's been jawin' away about all the fellers who wanted to marry her," the man explained in disgust. "I had to shut her up somehow, so I got into my clothes and got out of there. Bet she's still yappin' away. Once she gets started there isn't a damned thing can shut her up. Y'know, Cather, I've been married almost thirty years."

"Y'don't say! Thirty years, eh? That's a long, long time."

"Yeah, thirty years come September," the man continued. "But y'know something, Cather? After all them years I still don't know if I did the smart thing gettin' myself hitched or if I'd have been better off stayin' single. Oh, I'm willin' to give the devil his due and own up that a wife's a doggoned handy thing to have around."

"But?"

"Well, it seems there was one feller in particular who wanted to marry Dora, a drummer by the name of Honeywell, Francis Oliver Honeywell. He threatened to jump off a cliff if she turned him down. He was so doggoned pretty, all the girls fell for him. He never smelled of horses and such. Hell, no. He used some kind of stinkum, and when the girls got a whiff of him, they just fell at his feet."

"Did he jump off that cliff like he said he would?"

"Hell, no! He come past our place about three years afterwards, and from what I could see of him, he sure

138

looked beautiful. And did he stink! That stable of mine smelled a heap better to me. He didn't recognise Dora, didn't even give her a second look. For about a month afterwards Dora mooned around like a sick calf; then she started yappin' about Mister Honeywell all over again, and it's been goin' on ever since for twenty-seven years. Y'know, Cather, if anybody had the right to jump off a cliff, I'm the one."

They turned mechanically and strolled along.

"Got a brother of mine who married a squaw," the man began again. "He always was a smart one and I'm always willin' to give him credit for bein' smart. That squaw of his tends to everything, and never opens her mouth, 'cept maybe once or twice a day. Even when she does talk she don't say much, 'cause she only knows a handful of words and most of them are cuss words. But the point I'm tryin' to make is that she can do everything any other woman can do and do it without a peep. A woman like that's worth her weight in gold. Dammit, Cather, when that son of mine starts moonin' over girls, I'm gonna give him a talkin' to, and if he don't take it on the run to the nearest Injun camp, I'm gonna beat his brains out! Come on, man. I'll keep you company for the rest of the night."

CHAPTER X

THE DAWN SKY was drab and colourless when the train stirred into wakefulness. Here and there canvas curtains were whipped back, and yawning and sleepy-eyed people appeared, glanced skyward mechanically and climbed down to the ground. The guards stamped out their camp fires and, their rifles slung over their shoulders, came tramping up to the train and headed for their wagons.

Bill Raines was buckling on his gunbelt when Peggy opened her eyes.

"Morning, sleepy head," he said.

She stretched herself, looked up at him and smiled.

"Is it morning already?" she asked.

"Sure is," he answered.

She made a wry face, added a pout.

"And I was having the very nicest dream I ever had, and now I don't know how it ended."

He grinned at her.

"Well, suppose you turn over and go back to sleep while I'm fixing some coffee? Maybe you can pick up where you left off and see the thing out."

"Oh, Bill, I couldn't do that!"

"Why not?"

"Our first breakfast? I couldn't let you fix it. Why, what would people say?"

"The heck with them."

She considered for a moment.

"Of course," she said finally, a bit hesitantly, "if you insisted . . ."

He came to her side, knelt down, looked at her for a moment, bent over and kissed the tip of her nose.

"Go on," he said. "Turn over and get back to that dream. When the coffee's ready I'll call you."

She looked up at him, and a smile came over her face.

"You're sweet."

"Think so, hey?"

"Yes. And I'm awfully glad I married you."

"You keep telling me that and I won't be fit to live with," he said. "I'll get that swell-headed."

She reached up, drew him down to her and kissed him.

"There," she said. "You can get just as swell-headed as you please and I'll still love you. Bill, you're sure you don't mind fixing the coffee?"

"Nope."

She kissed him a second time, held his face in her hands for a moment, sighed, smiled again, and finally released him. Then she sank down, drew up the covers, turned over on her side and closed her eyes. He got to his feet and went out and climbed down from the wagon. He was hitching up his belt when there was a sudden rush of hooves. There was a woman's scream, a man's yell, and a deafening roar of gunfire. A bullet whined and ploughed through the wagon shaft, and a second one skimmed over the ground squarely between his feet. His Colt leaped into his hand. It snapped upward, steadied,

141

then it thundered twice as a quartette of horsemen bent low in their saddles came pounding past the wagon. The blast of gunfire lifted one man out of his saddle and sent him slumping earthwards. A horse directly behind him screamed with pain, stumbled to his knees and fell, pinning his rider beneath him. The man somehow managed to free himself, rolled away and had fought his way to his feet when the Colt belched flame and lead. The man tottered Another bullet hurled him to the ground, and he fell in a heap with his gun doubled up under him.

Raines leaped up on the wagon, dived over the driver's seat and hunched down behind it.

"Peggy!" he yelled without turning. "Stay down on the floor!"

Hastily he reloaded his gun, remembered that he had left his rifle just inside the wagon and reached for it quickly, grabbed it and laid it down at his feet, then levelled the Colt expectantly. He heard the pounding of hooves again and he knew the raiders were swinging back along the line of wagons. Raising his head cautiously and peering out, he caught a fleeting glimpse of a strung-out line of horsemen racing up the length of the train, saw flame belch from their guns. Rifle fire thundered in reply and he jerked his head down and waited. There was only a momentary wait. Hooves pounded past, and he peered out again and emptied the Colt into a group of horsemen. Quickly he holstered the Colt and caught up his rifle, levelled it and, when a lathered horse came into his sights, fired. The horse reared up and crashed over. The man in the saddle, riding with his feet free of the stirrups, rolled over, scrambled to his feet, whirled and snapped a shot at Bill. The rifle roared again and the man's face disappeared in a haze of gunsmoke. When it lifted a bit and Bill looked down, the man lay sprawled out on the ground.

Rifle in hand, Raines jumped down and huddled behind a wheel: He stole a quick look around him. Everywhere he looked, men with rifles or Colts in their hands were kneeling behind wagon wheels and firing through the spokes at their attackers. Again Raines reloaded his Colt and held it ready, but this time there was no clatter of hooves. There was a yell from somewhere far along the line.

"We got 'em!" he heard a man shout triumphantly. "We beat 'em off!"

He laughed and got up and holstered his gun. Will Cather came running up the line, a gun gripped in his pudgy right hand.

"You all right, boy?" he demanded pantingly. "You didn't get hit, did you?"

"No," Raines answered. "How'd we do?"

"Oh, we whittled them down all right. 'Less my eyes are seein' double, I'd say there's more than a dozen of them layin' out there in the grass that aren't ever gonna be of any use to McBride again."

"We ought to go after them," Raines said. "They won't be expecting it, and we might catch them and maybe finish them off. You hold the fort, Will, while I get the boys together."

He bolted away so quickly that Cather had no chance to say anything in reply. It seemed but a few minutes later when horsemen came riding out from in between wagons, spurred their mounts and rode down the line. Raines came sprinting back, saddled his horse, shoved his

143

rifle into the saddle boot and leaped up astride the animal.
He wheeled and raced away.

"Watch yourself!" Cather yelled after him, but Raines
did not answer.

There were twenty-six horsemen in the hastily recruited
force that awaited Raines. He ran his eye over them and
nodded. Tom Howell was among them. He grinned at
Raines.

"All right, men," the latter began briskly. "Here's our
plan. We're splitting up. Half of you go with Howell,
the rest of you with me. Tom, you and your men ride
westwards for about a mile, then swing in a circle southwards. We'll ride eastwards, then circle around to meet
you. Your horses ought to be rested enough for a good,
fast run, so let them out. I have an idea McBride's outfit
is pretty well shot up, and if that's so they won't be
looking for trouble. They'll be staying put licking their
wounds. I think maybe we can catch them between us
and really finish them off."

A murmur ran through the massed horsemen.

"If we have the luck to catch them between us," Raines
continued, "we'll close in on them on foot, with no man
taking any unnecessary chances, but still not holding back.
If my bunch runs into them first, we'll try to drive them
towards you. If your men, Howell, get to them before we
do, it will be up to you to push them into our hands. Or
our guns, I should have said. Anyway, that's the plan.
All right, Howell?"

"Yeah, sure," was the ready response. "Just say when."

"Twelve of you men will go with Howell," Raines instructed. "You other men will ride with me."

There was some confusion with some horsemen

wheeling this way, while others sought to go the other way. But shortly the two groups were formed. Howell, at the head of his group, twisted around, waiting eagerly for Raines' signal.

"Remember now, use your rifles," Raines reminded them. "No close quarters and no Colts. Go ahead."

"Let's go!" Howell yelled.

He dashed away and the men bunched together behind him, lashed their horses and pounded away after him. Raines led his band off to the east.

"By twos!" he called over his shoulder.

The strung-out line behind him became a more compact array as it formed into a two abreast alignment. With Raines setting a swift pace, the eastward mile was speedily negotiated. Suddenly Raines was turning and yelling again over his shoulder:

"Watch it!" We're swinging around!"

There was no discernible break in the band's pace. Swiftly it swung in an arc that carried it southwards and then westwards. Then the distant crack of a rifle reached eager ears. Every man's head jerked up. Howell had made contact with McBride's badly shot-up crew. Swelling rifle fire echoed over the dawn-lit range. Rifles were loosened in saddleboots. The pending excitement within the mounted men seemed to communicate itself to their horses, for they ran even faster than before. They topped a rise and panted to a stop when Raines barked a signal. A quarter of a mile away rifle flashes of red and yellow were stabbing the greyness.

"They're driving McBride towards us," Raines said shortly. "Let's go, but all of you be ready to dismount the minute I give the word. When I holler, get down, turn your horses loose and hit the ground on your bellies. Don't crowd one another. The more room there is between you and the man next to you, the less chance McBride's men will have of hitting anyone. All right. Let's ride."

They rode on again, stirrup to stirrup, each man with one foot free of its stirrup, ready to swing down the moment Raines gave the word. It came suddenly, even sooner than anyone expected. For suddenly, out of some billowing dust came a band of horsemen.

"Hey, there they are!" someone said excitedly.

Instantly all eyes focused on the emerging enemy.

"Dismount!" Raines called calmly and unhurriedly.

Fourteen legs swung over fourteen saddles and in a moment fourteen rifles were jerked free and gripped tightly. The horses were turned loose. They simply drifted back into the greyness behind their riders.

"Spread out," Raines called.

A couple of hundred feet to the south of McBride's outfit another band of horsemen appeared. It was Tom Howell's. McBride's men had halted, apparently uncertain for the moment as to which way to ride.

"There's about thirty of them," someone estimated.

"Yeah," another man confirmed the count, and added: "But we've got them where we want them. Right smack between us."

Rifle fire broke out as Howell's men, who had pulled up and dismounted, began to shoot. Rifle smoke swirled about them, hiding them briefly. Now McBride's men began to answer. Their Colt fire sounded far less authoritative than Howell's.

"Down on your bellies," Raines ordered, "and start

146

moving in on them. Fire!"

Half a dozen rifles thundered, then the volume increased as Raines' men, moving forward at a crawling
pace, settled down to the business at hand. The range
echoed with the swelling roar of gunfire. Smoke spun
around, lifted and drifted towards McBride's horsemen
and walled around them, screening them for the moment.

"Move in closer!" Raines yelled, and his sprawled-out
riflemen began to inch their way further forward. "Pour
it into them!"

The rifle fire reached a new high, and the ground
vibrated as a result of the leaden thunder. There was a
brief respite while empty guns were hastily reloaded. But
the interlude was short, and soon the ear-splitting din was
resumed. Howell's men were closing in, and Raines,
kneeling as he fired, took note of it.

"Spread out more!" he yelled. "Don't wanna give
them a chance to bunch up and break out!"

Three of McBride's horsemen sought to make a break
for freedom. Lashing their mounts they broke away from
the main body and flinging themselves forward against
their horses' necks came pounding down upon Raines'
men. Rifle fire sent two of the oncoming horses plunging
to the ground, and their riders, gaining their feet, wheeled
and scurried back. The third man survived the almost
point-blank shooting, as did his horse. He broke through
Raines' line and just when it appeared that he would suc-
ceed in making his escape, a couple of riflemen twisted
around and shot him off his horse. One of the riflemen
yelled triumphantly and turned himself around again. The
steady, merciless thunder of gunfire continued.

The trainmen's horses raised their heads occasionally

and watched the battle briefly; but their interest in it was shortlived and they turned their heads away.

The fire from Howell's men seemed to slacken off now; when it broke out again it was louder than before, a sign that they had moved even closer to their quarries. There was no need for Raines to urge his men to move closer. They crawled forward willingly, of their own accord too, poured volley after volley into the trapped men, reloaded and promptly resumed bracketing them with their deadly fire. Then it was over, so suddenly and abruptly that few of the men seemed to realise that they were drawing no answering fire from McBride's band. Those who did sense it, were doubly anxious to make certain that their hard-earned victory did not slip through their hands. They increased their fire, shooting at shadowy figures that were now barely visible in the haze of gunsmoke. They had no way of knowing that the men who were still astride their horses were dead, that they had died in their saddles and that the continued bullet riddling they were receiving was simply tearing them to bits. Raines was among the first to appraise the situation. He came leaping to his feet.

"Hold it!" he yelled. "Hold your fire!"

The fire along the curving line of riflemen slackened and finally died out, although for some minutes afterwards the carrying echo of gun thunder lingered in the air. The smoke that had been swirling around the bunched-together raiders began to lift. It billowed upwards in feathery clouds and after a short climb skywards dissolved into nothingness. The attackers got to their feet, their rifles lowered but still ready for instant use. Their eyes swept over the scene before them. Dead men and dead horses lay sprawled out in the lush grass, grotesquely twisted and broken. Wide eyes stared hard, held by the horrible fascination of the havoc they had wrought. They saw a raider's body slip sideways out of his saddle and topple to the ground; their eyes shifted and held on a second man who swayed and tumbled earthwards. Dull thumps indicated the toppling of a third and finally a fourth raider.

Raines had put down his rifle. Now he came striding forward. He circled a fallen horse, stopped here and there and peered into the faces of the dead men who lay about him. There was a sudden stirring, a movement, just beyond him, and he looked up instantly. There were two horses standing together some ten or fifteen feet away, with two men astride them, and both men slumped forward in their saddles. There seemed to be nothing unusual about them save that they looked 'dead.' He shook his head and turned away. He heard a strange, warning snort from one of the horses and instinctively flung himself sideways. A Colt roared at the same moment and a bullet ploughed the earth at his feet. The two horsemen sprung past him as he struck the ground and rolled away and slithered over on his stomach. He jerked out his gun and scrambled to his feet, wheeled around and snapped a couple of hastily fired, but badly aimed shots at the fleeing raiders. Out of a corner of his eye he saw a couple of trainmen run for their horses. But it was too late. The two apparently 'dead' men had come to life so suddenly, taking the trainmen so completely by surprise, they had broken through and made their escape. Raines cursed aloud.

A horseman came dashing up, pulled up squarely in front of Raines. The rider was Tom Howell.

"C'mon!" he yelled. "We can still get them!"

Another man, one of Raines' group, rode up.

"Get down," Raines said quickly.

The man looked blankly at him.

"Get down!" Raines cried.

The man swung himself out of the saddle. Raines fairly snatched the reins out of his hand, crowded him out of the way and vaulted up astride the horse. He wheeled the animal.

"Come on, Tom!" he flung over his shoulder.

Howell was at his side as they dashed away. They heard hoofbeats behind them, but they disregarded them. They wanted no assistance in disposing of the fugitives Lashing their horses, they sent them bounding over the range. They urged them on faster, drove them on by lashing them again with the loose ends of the reins. Just as the fight had ended so suddenly, it was with equal suddenness that they overtook their fleeing quarries. Actually it was Howell who spotted them. Riding with his left hand gripping the reins and his rifle clutched tightly in his right hand, he yelled suddenly, snapped the weapon upwards and fired.

"Got him!" he yelled excitedly.

He swerved southwards sharply, and Raines, following him, wheeled with him. A hundred feet away a horse lay threshing about in the grass. Just beyond him was a mounted man who was urging a lumbering man to run faster. Raines needed no closer view of them to know that the horseman was the gunman, Lopat, and that the big man who lumbered like a bear was the burly Mc-

150

Bride. He snapped a protesting shot at McBride who flung one back at him. Both went wide. Raines' horse stumbled and nearly threw him and Raines' second shot at McBride lost itself in flight too.

McBride reached Lopat's side. The gunman grabbed McBride's upthrust right hand and pulled hard, as if he thought he could haul the big man up behind him. Raines' Colt interfered; in fact a bullet from the big six-shooter struck Lopat's horse in a vital spot, and the animal cried out and sank to his knees. The swarthy killer kicked his feet free of the stirrups and leaped nimbly to the ground. He whirled and snapped a shot at the oncoming men. The bullet tore Howell's hat off his head, sent it spinning away. It finally dropped limply in the grass. McBride, turning, took a quick look, decided that to stand and fight meant death, and began to run. Lopat, however, stood his ground. He fired twice more, and Howell's horse cried out each time and finally stopped. His injured legs gave way beneath him and he fell. Howell cursed and got off him. Lopat laughed and had started away after McBride when Howell's rifle roared with an authoritative voice. The gunman staggered momentarily, steadied himself and turned around. His gun slanted upwards. There were two shots as Raines swerved away in pursuit of McBride. He stole a quick look over his shoulder. He saw Lopat spin and plunge face downwards into the grass; shifting his eyes he saw Howell sag and crumple up on the ground. He pulled up abruptly and wheeled as four horsemen came pounding up.

"Take care of Howell," he yelled. "I'm goin' after

McBride."

The men dismounted, ran to Howell's side and bent over him. Reluctantly Raines spurred his mount and darted away again. A bullet whined past his head and he bent low; a second bullet spun dirt in his horse's face. Raines decided he had had enough. He reined in and slid out of the saddle, whacked his horse on the rump, and the animal, snorting protestingly, wheeled and trotted back. A bullet ploughed the earth a foot to the left of him and Raines promptly twisted away. A fourth and then a fifth shot echoed, but missed him too. He skidded to a stop.

"All right, McBride," he panted. "This is it, y'know. It's pay-off time. You can use that last bullet on yourself. If you don't, when I get you, I'm gonna blast you apart. What'll it be?"

McBride did not delay in making up his mind. His last bullet drilled through Raines' hat, and the youth yelled and plunged forward. There was a scampering, and McBride suddenly appeared in front of him. He whirled and hurled his emptied gun at his pursuer. It sailed over Raines' head and fell to the ground. McBride bolted away. He had put some thirty feet between Raines and himself when the youth's Colt roared. McBride stumbled and fell. Raines waited patiently, and after a minute McBride forced himself up. His left arm hung limply against his side.

The Colt thundered a second time and McBride grunted and staggered. Now his right arm hung uselessly at his side. There was a stain of blood on his left shirtsleeve; now blood also dampened and darkened his right sleeve. McBride steadied himself, bracing himself on wide-spread legs. He raised his head, and moistened his lips with his tongue in a quick, darting, nervous gesture. The muzzle of Raines' Colt yawned and gaped at McBride's ample stomach and chest.

"In case you don't know it," Raines said. "We got Lopat."

McBride's eyes gleamed. He raised his head just a bit more. The Colt thundered in his face, and gunsmoke swirled around him. He was motionless for a moment; then he pitched forward and crashed on his face. Raines holstered his gun, turned on his heel and trudged away. The horse he had borrowed was munching grass some forty feet away. He turned his head and looked at Raines when the youth came striding up to him. He permitted Raines to mount, wheeled and loped off, quickening his pace without voicing a protest when Raines spurred him. They pulled up when they reached the spot where Howell had fallen. The men kneeling beside him looked up.

"How is he?" Raines asked quickly. "Hit bad?"

One of the men laughed.

"He's got a head on him that must be made of solid iron," he answered. "That bullet would've killed 'most anybody else. It just creased his skull. He'll be all right in no time at all."

* * *

The days and the weeks that followed were uneventful, but they were happy ones. A couple of guards were posted at night, but actually there was no great need for such precautions; nothing happened, no one appeared to disturb the calm, and after a while the guards themselves relaxed to such an extent that they simply rolled themselves up in their blankets at their appointed posts and went to sleep.

The train lumbered steadily westwards, and northern Nevada was a delight. The intense, gruelling heat of southern Wyoming and the oppressive air of Utah were memories now as they struck across Nevada with Virginia City directly ahead of them. Eyes never turned from the west; everyone's thoughts were of the promised land that was now but a scant couple of hundred miles away.

They were probably three days' travel from Virginia City when someone called Will Cather's attention to a dust cloud some distance behind them that was coming towards the train at a rapid pace. Rifles were hastily snatched up, the women and children were hustled into the depths of the wagons and ordered to lie flat on the wagon's floor, then a line of outriders was quickly formed and sent out, with Raines riding at its head. Faces that had learned to relax in those happy weeks grew grim and tight-lipped again. Then a rhythmic pounding of hooves swelled and caused a general catching of everyone's breath.

A long line of blue-clad horsemen riding two abreast swept along the train, and a slim, sun-bronzed officer with a cavalry sabre swinging against his left leg came whirling up to the head of the train, rode around the Anderson wagon, spotted Cather riding in advance of it, pulled up alongside him and snapped a salute. A flag-bearer clat-

tered up, and everyone's heart pounded as never before
when the Stars and Stripes began to whip about in the
breeze. There was a yell of delight from somewhere in
the train.

"Pull up!" Cather ordered, twisting around.

The train ground and braked to a stop. A handful of
young officers, and a couple of grizzled men who Cather
promptly decided were scouts, rode up and reined in.
Cather relaxed.

"Howdy," he said heartily.

The first officer acknowledged the greeting with a smile.

"Troop C and D, Fifth United States Cavalry," he said.
"I am Major Steele, commanding."

"I'm Will Cather."

They shook hands gravely.

"What are you fellers doin' out here?" Cather asked.

"We're *en route* to California," the Major answered.
"We're to establish a garrison at Fresno."

Cather's eyes widened.

"Y'don't say!"

"I take it you're headed that way, too," Steele continued. "With your permission, we'd like to go along with
your train. Of course," and he laughed, "we've a purpose in doing that. Our rations are running a bit low,
and perhaps you might be willing to sell us some of your
supplies."

"We've got enough bacon to supply an army," Cather
replied, "and you fellers are welcome to as much of it as
you can eat."

"Splendid," Major Steele said.

"Only we haven't got any to sell. My people wouldn't

hear of sellin' you fellers anything. Look, long's we've stopped, how about joining us in a bite now, huh?"

"Thank you," Steele said. "Thank you very much."

"Forget it," Cather said. He turned in his saddle. People from the wagons were crowding around, and Anna and Katey Heydrich were among them. "Missus Heydrich," he called.

Anna came forward, and Katey followed, stopping a bit behind her. Anna smiled as she came up.

"Major Steele," Cather said, "I'd like you to meet Missus Heydrich. The pretty girl behind her is her daughter Katey."

Steele's right hand snapped to the brim of his dust-streaked campaign hat.

"Missus Heydrich," Cather went on, "how'd you like to have the Major and maybe one of his officers eat with you people?"

Anna smiled delightedly.

"We would like it very, very much," she answered. She turned quickly. "Katey, you will take care of these gentlemen, please, while I go see about things. Yes?"

Major Steele dismounted. He beckoned to one of his officers, a tall, good-looking youth who swung himself out of the saddle, stepped forward briskly, and saluted.

"Miss Heydrich," Steele said, and Katey's cheeks showed a tinge of crimson. "May I present Lieutenant Webster?"

"How do you do," Katey said.

"Your servant, Ma'am," Webster said, saluting again.

"Webster," the Major said, "suppose you go along with Miss Heydrich. I want a few words with Mr. Cather;

then I'll follow you."

Train people backed off to permit Katey and the tall young officer to pass through.

*　*　*

Hustling about, with Anna urging him on, Kurt Heydrich placed four short lengths of board on the grass near their second wagon, and Anna quickly spread a tablecloth over the boards.

"It is one of your best," Kurt said, looking at it. "No?"

Anna smiled.

"I have never used it before," she said. "Kurt, Fresno, California—have you ever heard of it?"

"Fresno?" he repeated. "There is such a place?"

"Oh, yes."

"You know someone who lives there?"

Anna smiled again, deeply.

"Anna," Kurt said, "when you smile like that, I know you are up to something. What is it?"

"Nothing, Kurt, nothing," she said quickly. "It's—well, I was wondering how it would be there, you know, for us to live there."

"I see. Who is the young man who lives there?"

Anna laughed.

"His name may be Steele," she said. "Or it may be something else. His exact name I do not know; that is, yet. But if I tell you something, you will not be angry with me, will you?"

"First you must tell me."

"There is to be a fort in Fresno," she said. "These officers are to command it. Perhaps . . . "

"I see. So Mama is again making plans for her daughter."

Anna did not answer.

"I suppose it will always be like that," Kurt mused, "as long as there are mothers with marriageable daughters."

Anna stepped past him, turned and looked quickly up the line of wagons. There were blue-uniformed men everywhere.

"Kurt," she said, and he came to her side. "Look. There is Katrina now. You see her, with that tall young officer? See how she looks up at him, how she listens to everything he says, and now how she laughs? Kurt, have you ever seen her happier?"

He shook his head.

"Well, Kurt, shall we go to Fresno?" she asked with a smile.

He hitched up his belt. "The silverware and the dishes," he said. "I will get them."

He climbed up into the wagon, disappeared inside for a moment, reappeared presently and handed them down to her. He watched her as she went about setting the improvised table. He saw her lips move; then he smiled contentedly as he heard her singing.

THE END